THE WHITE SHOES

DAVID CAMACHO COLÓN

Rare Seed
10 Campo Bello
Guaynabo, PR, USA 00969

www.loszapatosblancos.com

ISBN (Paperback): 978-0-9903121-2-3
ISBN (eBook): 978-0-9903121-3-0

To Carmen S.

CHAPTER I
Ferrous the wise

L ife is as it is because it is full of surprises. As I embark on the journey, I don't know if what awaits me is an existence with an abundance of luxuries such as caviar and coffee processed by the digestive tract of a Kopi Luwak, or if I will be rolling in shit like a pig in mud. I don't know whether I will win a Nobel for my grand contributions to the prosperity of mankind or if I will limit myself to surviving the banality of day-to-day life, complaining and making up excuses for what I don't have, for what I haven't done, and for whom I didn't manage to become.

Whatever. Those things were of little importance to me. I'm nothing more than a soul. What mattered was the body I was assigned! Neither my past lives nor the wisdom I gained in them would serve me if I didn't manage to connect with my current body. It was then that things got complicated because connecting with this pile of meat and bones not only meant operating all its parts and pieces, but also meant succeeding in influencing the conscious being living within it.

The early years of Ciprián's life, the being with whom I now share a body, were of adjustment and assimilation. It

1

was to be expected because the memories of my past lives obviously weren't his own. I kept those memories with me, not inside his brain; there was no physical connection between them. He couldn't extract them. I couldn't share them. Ciprián and his body needed to start from scratch, on a clean slate like everybody else.

There was little I could do during those early years, at least not until Ciprián himself built an adequate database of useful memories. Most of the time he was on autopilot mode, at the mercy of those around him: his family. They were in charge of giving him his first memories, teaching him how to survive, sharing with him their principles and morals.

Although tedious, these were inevitable stages for me to pass through. When my past life came to an end, my body died an antiquated old man whose state was considered useless and repulsive. What good would I have done if I had gotten control over Ciprián right from the beginning of his physical existence? Life is so different among cultures and can differ so much between generations. My early years in a body are restricted to observation and reflection as I get used to my new reality, so that I can get up to speed on what in my next life will inevitably be the ideas of an antiquated old man. Ciprián's family was useful not only to him, but also to me—at least until I was ready to be in charge of things.

Being the soul that I am, my sole responsibility was managing Ciprián's memories. I kept collecting and combining new memories with the old ones, strengthening some and weakening others in the process. Strong memories were especially useful as I could show them to him when he needed them most. They sparked in him an idea, a concept, a eureka moment, whatever was necessary to seize the moment and take on any challenge that was put in front of him. It was like playing a never-ending game of charades where I perpetually tried to help Ciprián guess correctly on his first try every time, so that he would always choose the most convenient path for himself.

Memories are somewhat complex, though. They come in packages, like sandbags, each memory with its own bag. The moment a memory is formed, each of the senses puts in its grain of sand. Joe Schmo may argue that visual memory is the most important. It is not because at the moment something is seen, something is also smelled, even if it's odorless; something is heard, even when there is silence; something is touched, even if it's the wind; and so it is with all the senses and sensors that the body has. Even mood, how happy or sad the person is feeling during that instant of life, contributes some grains to the memory bag. The more grains each sensor adds, the more memorable that memory becomes. The more memorable a memory becomes, the better my chances to help Ciprián guess, on his first attempt, any idea I have to give.

At the age of five, when he had already mastered the art of running without falling and sweeping the floor with his knees—at least when he didn't do it as often anymore— Ciprián stretched his body to the limits for the first time in his life. He couldn't help but be competitive. He had this insatiable thirst for imposing himself on others in everything. He was determined to demonstrate with one victory, regardless of how small or insignificant it was for him or for the world, that he was superior to anyone in both body and spirit. Victory was his only goal. At that moment, it didn't cross his mind that his adversary might or might not have felt that the situation merited giving it his all, that his adversary might not have seen defeat as a grave threat to his honor.

"Simón, come! Let's race!" Ciprián shouted, having already had half the starting line drawn with the heel of his foot. He suspected that his cousin of the same age would be an easy opponent to beat.

"OK! The loser is a girl!" Simón stuttered, giggling as he positioned himself behind the starting line. His feet, crucial to the slightest hope of success in the race, raged against the ground like a bull preparing to charge. In all truth, he was really only pawing up dust.

"On your marks, get set, go!" Ciprián said, strategically timing his every word, elongating some syllables and shortening others. They both shot out at the same time, Ciprián ahead by a micro-second because he knew the exact moment the race would start.

At that age, the small backyard of his house was an endless field for them. They ran alongside the patches of vegetables and spices that Flora, his mother, grew as stir-fry and seasoning ingredients for her dishes. The fiercest part of the race took place as they passed the tomato, onion, and garlic plants. Simón, taller and larger than Ciprián, kept clumsily throwing his body at him. It was impossible for Simón to run in a straight line. As they were reaching the achiote, cilantro, and bell peppers, Ciprián was ahead but still close enough to hear his cousin snorting like a pig. It wasn't until just before passing the parsley, cumin, oregano, and saffron plants that he looked over his shoulder to see if he had secured his victory. Dissatisfied with the gap in his favor, he pushed himself to the limit and set his sights on the finishing line. Before he could even realize it, he was already there. He was made aware of this fact by the gate made out of solid iron that he never saw.

When he woke up after some time, everything seemed hazy. He could still taste blood and rusted iron on his lips. The trauma was so severe that he didn't feel pain. He thought he had just gotten a bruise like the many others he had already survived despite his young age. It wasn't the case. The seismic impact, flesh clashing with iron suddenly and at full speed, left him with what resembled a geological formation on his forehead. A deep gorge originated there, extending from the limits of his skin to the depths of his cranial bones. From below the surface emerged warm and soft currents that, as they overflowed, trickled over the tiled floor.

Flora, his mother, a firm believer in ointments and home remedies, plastered his head with ingredients from her kitchen cupboard. Ciprián, his pain increasing as he regained consciousness, moaned uncontrollably.

"Sweetheart, just hold on for a teeny bit longer. The doctor is on his way. What a strong man you are; you don't even cry!" Flora said. "Simón, hold his head still while I look for the can of udder cream."

"What's that for?" Simón said.

"Well, first I'll put some salt on it to stop the bleeding. The udder cream is to stop the swelling," she said, as she applied the gunk of salt and udder onto her son.

Shortly after, the doctor arrived. He needed eight stitches to sew his head back together and effectively canalize the gorge. With that done, things went back to normal as if nothing had happened.

The memory of his clash against the iron gate is one of the oldest, yet one of the most pristine I have stored to this day. It is so because it is unique, incorruptible. It's not plagued by the impurities that the experiences of daily life leave on memories, those that smudge colors and distort shapes. It's not plagued by overly sad or overly happy feelings, those emotions with which memories incestuously pair up to beget offspring that strip the original memory of its authenticity. How often in his life would Ciprián strike his head, involuntarily and at full speed, against an iron gate? I wouldn't be able to spoil such a unique memory even if I wanted to.

Some years later, Ciprián found himself in a situation surprisingly similar to that of his encounter with the iron gate. As before, it was a race with his honor and glory at stake, on this occasion against a friend from school. He was flying. His opponent was not a serious threat, despite the fact that, unlike his cousin, this one could run in a straight line. Just as it had happened years before, he couldn't resist the temptation to look back, all to ensure victory and savor the memory. The two scenarios were so similar that he instinctively made the right choice in the game of charades. It only took that one vivid memory to make Ciprián look forward early enough and avoid a collision. For one thousandth of a second, Ciprián grinned, feeling he had just prevented a disastrous accident from taking place.

However, the lesson that we both learned at that moment was the importance of the friction between the turf over which one runs—in this case polished cement—and the soles of one's shoes—smooth by design and fabrication—to abruptly come to a halt at such speeds. Thanks to me Ciprián saw the lonely bench that stood one meter in front of the finishing line, but as he attempted to halt, he slipped and fell on his ass.

Because the fall wasn't the result of halting as much as it was of his slipping, he was thrust forward by his own inertia and slid under the bench, which was made of solid concrete, fifteen centimeters thick. Two miserable centimeters of his head located in the bone between the right eyebrow and the right eye, could not be spared. They collided against the most unyielding corner of the bench.

"This is the third handkerchief I bathe in your blood this year alone," Mr. Rodríguez said, as he carried him in his arms and walked briskly to the infirmary. Unfortunately for him, it was his duty to watch students play during recess.

Ciprián, so lightheaded that he was incapable of responding, only managed to look into Mr. Rodríguez's eyes, which were grossly magnified given the exaggerated thickness of his glasses.

Despite his fatal clashes against stationary objects, his childhood still fit within the parameters of normalcy. He grew up in the countryside, where there was no place for the word 'boredom'. When he and his friends weren't sliding downhill, riding on top of palm tree leaves, they were coming up with ingenious designs for home-made toys. This has already become a lost art. It came from a world where buying toys was much more of a privilege than an obligation. They got raw materials from anywhere. The all-terrain trucks with which they played on the ground, for example, were made from pieces of wood that formed the body and four nails that worked as axles. The wheels attached were no more than Vienna sausage cans taken from Flora's kitchen.

For the water, they built steam-powered boats. They attached a straw to a used can of shoe polish and used a candle to boil the water inside the can. The straw then served to release the steam that propelled the boat forward. They only needed to mount the engine onto anything that floated, and presto, on it went.

For the windy days, each built his own kite made out of paper and wooden sticks. They flew them just for fun, but naturally things always got more interesting when some sort of competition took place. Those competitions progressively evolved, from simply determining who could fly a kite the highest or for the longest time, to the more popular kite wars. In that game, the last kite left in the air was the winner. The only way to win was by taking down without compassion the kites of adversaries. To compete at this level, kites needed to be equipped with weapons that were both light and effective, minimizing the negative effects that any additional weight had on agility and reach. What better weapon for this purpose than razor blades?

"I have no issues with you guys flying those kites, but those razor blades need to go, starting today. Is that clear, son?" Augusto told Ciprián in his usual, calm tone.

"Those things will come loose and take somebody's eye out!" Flora shouted from inside the kitchen.

"OK! OK!" Ciprián replied. He didn't want to commit to obeying orders he knew he wouldn't follow, but in those days orders were orders; they couldn't be challenged.

He didn't feel it was fair. It was Augusto, himself, his father, who taught him how combat in kite wars and the tactics required, which earned him his reputation among friends. Besides, taking somebody's eye out? Seriously? What were the odds? Zero. Disobeying his parents, he continued playing the war games in secret.

One afternoon, however, due to an obvious streak of luck, Simón managed to destroy all the kites in the air. It was a strong blow to Ciprián's reputation and stature as champion. Simón, euphoric after finally winning for the first time in his life, didn't realize that one of the razor blades had fallen from the sky and was stuck deep into his arm. It wasn't until he felt his hands wet from the stream of blood rushing out that he took notice of the unbearable pain it caused.

CHAPTER II
Guava-flavored incentives

S imón was more like a brother to Ciprián than a cousin. He often ate and slept over at Flora's house. In those days, it wasn't unusual to raise other people's children. Flora was also more than glad to do it, as she never managed to have more than one child.

Flora had four brothers and one sister. Three of those brothers and her only sister chose to marry among cousins. Flora and her older brother decided to resist the family urge to share the same blood and found partners outside their family tree. Of the sprouts that emerged from those incestuous marriages, some came with malformations and mental problems. Three of them died shortly after being born.

Simón was one of the sprouts that survived. He wasn't really able to move the right side of his face. He couldn't smile like others or speak as well as others. His right leg was also crooked, limiting his ability to walk and run. Ciprián didn't notice these things until he had grown up some more, effectively dismissing his glorious victory at age five in which so much of his blood was spilt. Nevertheless, Simón compensated for his right-sided deficiency with his left side, with which he portrayed himself as giggly and cheerful as any other child. Just by looking at him, many people thought that Simón was weak, somewhat dumb, and incapable of being of any use. He really wasn't.

The day of Simón's accident with the razor blade, Augusto came home from work while Ciprián peacefully tended the chickens. Ciprián saw him go to the far end of the backyard, where the guava tree stood. He observed as his father pulled out a branch from the tree, one not more than a meter long, and started to pick out the leaves, letting them drop to the ground one by one. He then saw how he inspected the branch, making sure it was completely bare. He took just about long enough for his delicate ritual to be witnessed by the spectator of his choosing.

"Chepo, come here," his father called calmly.

"I'm coming!" Ciprián said, wondering what all the suspense was about.

Augusto grabbed him by the wrist with one hand and, with a surprise attack, gave him a beating.

"What have I been telling you about that damn game?" Augusto shouted, as he whipped him with the bare branch.

The mystery surrounding that guava tree branch was revealed that same instant. He bore witness as his own father became unempathic, carrying out his duty to discipline him when he messed up badly, while savoring the sadistic nature of his ritual. He knew what he was about to do, but he took his time to prepare calmly so that he could consciously implant terrible memories into the brain of his victim, his son.

Ciprián would bear witness to the ritual only a few times in his life, as it was normally Flora who was in charge of maintaining discipline. She went straight to the point during those moments while Augusto took on the role in a more strategic manner. The mere memory of the sting Ciprián felt as the guava tree branch caressed his legs was enough to set him straight; he could never predict how grave an offense needed to be in order to trigger the brutal ritual.

What Augusto knew about life, he learned from working the fields. As was the case with his siblings, he was the product of both his parent's love and their view children as being an investment. What better source of cheap and trustworthy labor than a son? Augusto never attended school because those days none existed. He had to work the land as soon as he could hold a machete. To harvest sugar cane there was no need to learn how to read or write, so he never did. He did learn his arithmetic well. That's how, as an adult, he made sure nobody took advantage of him; it's all it took to earn a living as a plantation overseer.

As Ciprián got older, he had to learn to do something other than play in the dirt with Simón. Augusto started by teaching him how to work with his hands. With some wood and a roll of chicken wire, they began by building a chicken coop and a corral.

"Once you have your design ready, you need to make sure you mark your measurements correctly on the wood before making your cut. You need to trace straight lines. Measure two times, three times, four times, as many as you need to be sure you're getting it right. Here, cut this one," Augusto said, once he finished tracing the cutting line. "Just make sure the wood doesn't move. You need to hold it steady. Keep the saw straight. You start cutting toward yourself first and then continue forward. It's easier that way. And make sure that you're always keeping an eye on the line you traced. Keep the saw straight and follow the line. Piece of cake! If you don't keep it straight it will get stuck and you won't get a clean cut," he added little by little to his lesson as he watched Ciprián struggling to complete the cut.

Once the corral was ready, Augusto brought two fat chickens and threw them inside. With the same patience he showed when teaching him how to work wood, he taught him how to keep the coop and the corral clean and how to protect the chickens from predators. He also borrowed a rooster to show him how to get more chickens and, some weeks after, how to take care of the nine chicks that hatched out of the eggs. Within a short time, and with the expert tutelage of his father, Ciprián had managed to master the foundations of raising and breeding chickens.

After a few months, Augusto selected the fattest and happiest hens and left them in the coop, then put the rest of the chickens in a box. He left early in the morning to sell them at the worker's market. He came back home that evening with some coins and a box of guava pastries for Ciprián. His reward was well received considering that far from substantial, it was more than he was used to getting.

"Dad, if I raise more chicks, can we sell them?" Ciprián said. His mouth was covered in confectionery sugar. His teeth made their way through the thin, crisp puff pastry layers until reaching its sweet, guava paste baked filling.

"We'll see," Augusto said.

The following day, his father came home with his neighbor's rooster. He had purchased it from him.

"With those hens you have, you can get two dozen eggs per week. With this rooster, you can get six dozen eggs per week within about six months. You should be able to get ten dozen eggs within eight months. What do you think? Can you handle it by yourself?" Augusto asked.

"Of course I can!" Ciprián answered immediately. He had no idea if that was possible, but as he believed himself to be an expert already, there was no way to make him reconsider his chances for success.

"Alright, so from next week on, you quit school and stay home," Augusto said.

"But, how much will I earn from working?" Ciprián asked, realizing what he was getting himself into. He expected a generous sum.

"You get the love that your mother and father already have for you because you are such a good son, as well as food and a roof over your head," Flora answered before Augusto could. Her tone made clear that she didn't agree he should quit school, but the decision was final.

He would never forget those words, be it because the whole idea of working for the wellbeing of the family sounded so altruistic, or because it had become Flora's automatic response to any request for money or reward, or because, at that moment, Flora was holding a lively guinea chicken in her hands. She pet it as she sermoned Ciprián. It began to get comfortable. Then, in front of Ciprián, she held its neck with her two hands and attempted to break its neck with a firm tug. She couldn't help her hands from slipping. Instantly the guinea chicken, having been betrayed and now suffering from a wobbly neck, screeched in agony as it tried to escape. Flora, a woman of strong character, didn't hesitate,

14

grabbed it by the neck with one hand, and spun it four or five times in the air, legs up, in the style of the *burlesque*.

The topic of remuneration was never again discussed.

His responsibilities were no longer the same as those he had before: limited to collecting eggs, feeding the chickens, and cleaning up poop. That was honest work but purely manual. His new role asked for more brains. He had egg deliveries to make per the weekly quotas his father had set for him.

When he started he had four laying chickens, which at roughly an egg a day got him just over two dozen eggs per week. They weren't enough! He knew he needed the rooster if he wanted to get more. He would only get to ten dozen eggs with about twenty chickens. He put the rooster to work all week to get at least forty fertilized eggs so that, with luck, at least half of them would be hens.

The coop was overflowing with eggs. Where would he put them after they hatched? The coop and the corral, made for four chickens, came nowhere close to being the size they needed to be to host the forty or fifty chickens he needed to raise. He had to act fast. To his relief, Simón, who had nothing else to do, was willing to be his apprentice.

It took a long time before he was able to meet his weekly quota. For Augusto that was unacceptable. When it came to business he was demanding and hard. He had let Ciprián fail because it was part of the learning curve. Now he was talking about disappointing clients, reducing his weekly income, and losing investments of time and money. He gave him no more chances, especially when he saw that so many of his problems were avoidable.

"How is it my fault that the chick didn't hatch? Or that it doesn't want to eat? Or that it got sick? Look! Sometimes they even kill each other!" Ciprián said, pointing his finger at a chicken with a featherless neck. It was running like crazy around the corral.

"You better figure those things out soon! All I see is a coop full of shit with a corral filled with holes this big, where rats as big as a rabbit can get through. You guys are doing something wrong," Augusto said, opening his arms much wider than the real size of one of the holes in the corral.

There was no room for excuses. Ciprián and Simón had to be ingenious when it came to compensating for the chickens that should have hatched but didn't, for those that were born weak and stupid, for the sick and contagious, and for the blood-thirsty cannibals that pecked each other to death.

Ciprián thought about those chickens day and night. He wasn't concerned about their miserable lives, which consisted of kicking straw, eating, and pooping; they lived their lives only to be fried or become soup, among other cooking methods. Whatever feelings a chicken could have likewise didn't make him lose sleep. Chickens, apart from staring at him without blinking, weren't very expressive, so to speak. He didn't sleep because his father's demands made him rack his brain until he found a solution to his problems. In other words, he put me to work overtime.

He enjoyed being stressed like that; it gave him pleasure. He also enjoyed having his family depend on him. He was contributing something to them. Maybe he took Flora's manipulative words too literally and thought that the love his parents had for him would be measured in eggs per week.

16

Speaking of love, Ciprián had his first discussion about the topic with his parents probably in the optimal setting, the kitchen. This is where all ingredients coincide at the right place, the right time, and in the right proportions to delight.

"This little girl mistreated me, despised me," Augusto said, as he put aside the green bananas he had just grated, picked up a tannia, and pondered for a few seconds. "You know what? I thought she would never give me a chance. I tried everything! I brought her flowers and she rejected them. I brought her chocolates and, well, those she liked so she didn't return them, but she took them halfheartedly. That didn't even get me more than one or two words, either. At first, I thought that would be it; getting her chocolates would be enough to get her to open up to me, but she was devious and all she wanted was more chocolates. I even wrote her dozens of love letters declaring my love for her, telling her how beautiful she was, how happy she made me feel, that she was my all and my everything," he said, as he kept adding pumpkin pieces and specks of salt and achiote oil to the mix.

"Blah, blah, blah. That was all it was," Flora interrupted him, trying not to smile. Meanwhile, sitting at his side, she caressed his neck. She then stood up and took a pot of pork stew out of the fire, took the lid off and stirred it with a spoon, then let two drops fall on her wrist to taste. The fragrance took over the whole kitchen. "Alright, this is ready. We'll let it sit for a bit and then we'll prepare the *pasteles*," she said, as she hovered over the fire some banana leaves that Ciprián had brought from the backyard.

"What did you do, then?" Ciprián asked.

"Well, that's the thing. I didn't know what to do! You just heard her reaction; that's what I always got! Blah, blah, blah!" Augusto said, making faces to mock Flora. "Can you imagine my frustration? Me, a young man in love, trying to have a serious conversation with her, trying to make her understand how she made me feel, but she didn't want to hear it! They were real feelings, you know? Anything I would throw at her, she would swing right back at me with that damned 'blah, blah, blah'. She thought I wasted my time doing this with every girl, that she was only one of many to whom I lied," he added, as he set up a production line for the *pasteles*. He was in charge of laying the mix for each *pastel* over the banana leaves and adding an olive and a red pepper, while Flora added the meat and Ciprián closed them up into a brick shape and tied them with thread. "That's when I came up with the idea of writing her a song," he said, raising his index finger and pointing it at his head. "I basically told her the same things I had written in the letters, but adding some rhythm to it seemed to cast a spell over her. What do you think about that? Ha, ha," he said, looking at Flora with a long grin and slapping her thigh with an open hand.

"But, if he was telling you practically the same things as on the letter, what difference did it make if he wrote it or sang it? Wasn't it the same?" Ciprián said to Flora, confused by the apparently contradictory behavior of her past self.

"There is a huge difference! Anybody off the street with one or two bucks to spare can get flowers and chocolates. In his letters, he wrote nice things but he was just putting on paper whatever came out of his head. That wasn't much different than coming up to me and spitting out all his lies," Flora said, as she boiled the *pasteles* Ciprián had just tied up.

"Right. It's the same with a song; it's on paper too," Ciprián said.

"Well, you're mistaken! Do you want to know why they're different? Because, even if he's writing the same thing, he has to put more work into it. He has to be more confident of what he writes. He has to think more about everything. He has to think more about which words he will use. The words won't just be whatever comes out of his head, but now they have to rhyme and sound beautiful. He can't lie to me anymore. He has to make sure I won't think he could use his song with any other random girl. He has to tailor-make it for me," Flora said, and then squeezed one of his cheeks and began wiggling it from side to side. "The more time he put into that song, the more he really thought about me. The more he thought about me, the more lies he forgot. I didn't even need to hear the song for the spell to be cast. That day he came to sing it, he had stopped looking at me with the seducing eyes of Don Juan and had begun looking at me with the sweet eyes of Don Augusto. This lazybones had really fallen in love with me."

It's hard to argue with that. From the beginning, Augusto had both the recipe and the ingredients, but he had to put some effort into learning how to cook and put more attention to details. Perhaps another girl would have feasted on those first plates he 'cooked', but not Flora; she had a more refined taste. She didn't eat just anything on her plate.

A few minutes after, Flora took out one of the *pasteles* and put it on a plate. She cut the thread and carefully unfolded the banana leaves.

"Here, try this," Flora said.

19

The aroma came to him through his nose and mouth; it tempted him until he was finally able to savor it. The outer layer of the *pastel* was thin and soft to the bite, giving way to a melody of meat and spices within its filling. Each ingredient played its note. Many excelled as part of a great symphony, others so enticing that they deserved their own *solo*. What genius must have existed within the heart of that great master who allowed such a worthy plate to be created?

CHAPTER III

Help from beyond

Margarita's diary: October 16, 1942

Weeks have passed and the dead man is still in my home. I don't know who that man is or why he's here. Every morning, I wake up with him stuck in my head. No matter where I'm headed, I know that as soon as I exit my room I'm bound to run into him. There is no way around it; I have to go through the living room in order to get anywhere else in the house. There is no other option except to turn into a lizard, climb up the walls of the house, and use the windows as doors. I shout at him, "Go away! Go!" He doesn't answer. He doesn't give me the subtlest of gestures to somehow tell me, "Yes, I see you are there, but I'm not interested in going anywhere. I want to keep annoying you!" At least that would give me a clue of what he's up to. He's in the living room, sitting on the sofa against the wall, with a portrait of none other than Jesus Christ hanging above his head. I don't dare to touch him; I would die!

He remains still, eternally dressed in his impeccable penguin suit. He wears a carnation corsage in his chest pocket and ivory white gloves. He's ready for an ultra-formal wedding, or God forbid, a runaway from his own funeral decades back. His shoes: like a mirror. The black hat: never without it. It's all a farce, a disguise, his groomed moustache included. He attempts to hide the paleness of his skin, the lugubriousness of his face, his damned sinister eyes. His specter was implanted inside my head. It follows me. Colorless flashes of those bloodcurdling eyes, visions, large and small, make rounds inside my head. They beat inside me and keep me awake. I'm terrified of them.

Although it has been difficult, I'm trying to deal with him. When I need to cross the living room, I simply run from one end to the other covering my eyes with my hands. Naturally, I make sure I can see a little bit between my eyes so I don't bump myself against the walls! I learned that lesson the hard way, with pain. If I don't run, then I stick my chest against the wall like a leech and I snail away until I reach the kitchen. That's how I stay alive.

If for any reason I must stay in the living room, what I do is to have my back to him. That way I don't have to look at him. I don't mind having him that close because I'm sure he won't move from there. All I want is to get him away from my eyes and my head! I'm stupid, though. I torture myself. No matter how determined I am, it's impossible for me not to look back every single minute. Covered in goosebumps, I look impatiently between my fingers for his blurry shape to confirm that he's still there, fully aware that all I'm doing is feeding my hysteria.

I know the man won't move from his place as long as it's daytime; evenings, however, are another story. He likes to wander around the house as if he owned the place. I sometimes look for him but can't manage to find him anywhere. That means he's hiding in some dark corner waiting to startle me. Darkness is a scary enough thing to also need to be worrying about the whereabouts of that man.

His favorite nocturnal resting place is in the kitchen, sitting on a chair at the table just beside the fridge. Not even moonlight reaches there. I can only make out the silhouette of his body, his black hat, and two faint dots of light that come out of his eyes and sparkle as they meet mine. He doesn't take his eyes away from me! I stand frozen for too long, lacking the will to give a step forward. All I can do is go back to my room and weep.

Mom and dad keep saying there's nothing there. They still can't see him. I know I'm not crazy. I see him. Why can't they see him as well?

Some days ago, dad grabbed an old pot and started stabbing it with a machete. He put some things inside, some mix of ingredients I don't recognize but I know came from the town market. There's one of those spiritist *botánicas* there. Before putting the lid on the pot, he lit up the mix and waited until white smoke came out through the perforations. It smelled of sweet incense. He carried the pot with some chains he had attached to its surface, which also served to keep the lid in place, and he let the whole thing hang from his hand like a swing. With no rush, he swung it back and forth, sprinkling smoke toward the direction it swung. He strolled around the house like so, filling with smoke every room and every corner, especially all doors, windows, and the perimeter of the house.

Dad told me that the smoke helped chase away evil spirits. That's exactly what mom said when I asked her about the mix she poured over the water she used to mop the floor. They want the house to be evil-spirit-proof, but smoking up the house and cleaning the floor with *riegos* was only the beginning. We have to chase away existing spirits, scare away others that want to come in, and take care of anybody who might be sending them here.

Mom and dad know of many protections that can be placed all around the house; that way they deal with this problem from all angles. They hung a small mirror from the roof of the front porch. According to them, mirrors reflect and prevent any evil coming from the outside. They also nailed small crosses made from purging nut tree branches to the walls, at all entry points of the house, and over the doors of every room inside, including the kitchen and the living room. Purging nut tree branches are said to stop any spirit from entering.

My room has been mined with papers full of scribbles in pencil that were then folded and hidden inside drawers, under my clothes, and under the mattress. In some odd way, the scribbles are supposed to make spirits realize that they are spirits and make them stop bothering people. However, mom says the protection from those scribbles is limited. Each piece of paper has a validity period, be it days or weeks. Upon reaching their expiration date, they'll need to be burnt and replaced in the case the man still hasn't left.

To protect me from the evil eye mom got me a jet stone, which I carry around in my pocket when I go anywhere. She also wrote my name on some small pieces of paper, which then ended up buried within a glass container full of sugar and suspended within another container full of honey. According to her, they are some sort of spiritual medicine to make me better.

As it could never be ruled out that somebody looking to harm me could have put a spell on me, remedies for that purpose had to be prepared. It didn't hurt to have them. Dad peeled a coconut, took out all the water on the inside, and placed it outside to dry under the sun. He took a brown piece of paper, wrote my name in pencil, folded it a few times, and stuck it inside the coconut. Unaware of what was going on, I got in the car with him and we went up to an intersection where four streets met. It was there that dad took out the coconut and smashed it against the gravel. I got so frightened! The coconut was in pieces. Dad said that breaking the coconut also broke any spell anyone might have had against me.

They have even poured some stuff over my body to make sure that man goes away; they call it a *mejunje*. I shower as I always do, with water and soap, but now mom and dad also bathe me with that thing. I don't like it because I feel like the smell of herbs, potions, and candles for saints they sell at the *botánica* is sticking to me. They tell me that I need to have patience and that I need to keep bathing with that stuff for many days until the man disappears. As they bathe me, they pray, recite the rosary, and command the spirit to go away, pleading to God to take him away. At the end of each bath, they take all of the *mejunje* that was used and they throw it down the latrine, a place nobody else will step on, to guarantee that anything that has come out of me has been permanently purged.

Mom suspects that it's one of those spirits that hasn't wanted to go to heaven because it believes that it still has something to do here in the world of the living, that there's someone to help. She says that not all of those spirits who stay here are bad or are looking to harm anyone on purpose; instead, they try so hard to help the living that, because they are not pure beings, they do harm them. I don't know about those things, but what I do know is that after all of the protections they've prepared for me I feel nothing different or magical. What I do hope is that the man can hear us and leaves soon. I want him to stop helping me!

I trust my mom, and I'm not the only one. Many people trust their secrets to her even if they don't know her. They come to visit her from all corners of the island because they want to ask her things. They all want to know what is coming to them with regards to money and businesses they have started. They come with jealousy attacks and want to know if their partners are being unfaithful, or they want to look for ways to make someone fall in love with them. They want to make headaches, leg pains, back pains, and all the rest of those aches and pains that come with age go away. Naturally, many come to dispel bad vibes, spells, and spirits, such as the man I see.

Mom's doors are always open to anybody wanting to visit. She does it gladly and refuses to charge for it. According to her, this gift God gave her was meant to help others, not to live a life of luxury in his name. For her, those mediums who ask for money are not blessed. They want money they don't need. They are frauds. They don't do what God has confided in them to do.

I haven't asked her too much about how her gift works, but I've seen things. I know she's able to read fortunes in two different ways. The first way is by walking down the street. She runs into any random stranger, man or woman, then suddenly stops them and stares deeply at their eyes. As if she had known them for many years, she takes them by an arm and begins to talk with them.

Those encounters are the most superficial ones. They are limited to giving small warnings to prepare for what's coming, so they can know who is looking to harm them or which of their projects in life will be successes or failures, but with few additional details. The most heartwarming thing I saw her do was when she put her hand over the belly of a pregnant woman and revealed to her that she would have a strong and healthy baby girl. The woman cried of excitement. She told my mother that she had already given birth to four boys and she desperately wanted a baby girl.

Those who come visit her get a more in-depth reading. They start gathering early in the morning in a waiting room like they would do when visiting the doctor, but sitting on some benches dad built under the open air. Mom stays with each of her visitors from ten minutes to an hour; she decides. She takes out a paper and pencil and starts asking questions, jotting down notes as they answer.

They aren't just any type of notes. What she writes is not in a legible language. She writes line after line of scribbles, the language of spirits. She can cover a full sheet with that unrecognizable gibberish. What's truly impressive is witnessing how she takes that same paper covered in hieroglyphics and she reads the person's fortune in such a casual and fluent manner. She assures me that what she writes on that paper is only what the spirits tell her from within her head, but that doesn't explain how she can read what she writes.

She once told me that I had been born with the hands to do these kinds of things but not in the same way. I won't be able to read anyone's fortune or cure with blessings and medicinal plants as she does. My gift would be that of seeing things through dreams and thoughts. All I can say is that if I'll be blessed with visions like the horrendous man sitting on the sofa, I care little for any gift God has in store for me. I don't need blessings of that sort in my life.

CHAPTER IV

I let you win

G ala, at the tender age of 14, had the body of a proper deity. She carried herself elegantly around town on her slim, straight legs, a perfect mold spanning from her ankles to her thighs. Her curves, hand carved along knee, calf, and ankle, subtly emphasized not only the delicacy of her figure, but also granted her with intense presence. The streets worshipped her. She knew how to walk. She toyed innocently—but with unmatched skill— with that line that separated what was decent from what was suggestive, what was fine from what was vulgar.

"Hey Ciprián, can you give me a ride to the city square?" Gala asked.

It was Gala, a muse with a youthful voice and chestnut curls, standing in front of him. The sparkle of her dark and wide eyes penetrated deeply into Ciprián's, in intriguing contrast with the appealing seriousness of her lips. She surprised Ciprián who was squatting on the street, busy ratcheting up the greasy nuts of his bicycle's wheels.

"Alright, let's go. You must be suffering, aren't you?" Ciprián said, seeing how her feet were being sawed off by the straps of her sandals, which were falling apart from walking so much.

He had met her not long before that day, not long after he noticed she wasn't a little girl anymore. At twenty-five years old, he wouldn't miss the rare chance to have such a specimen mounted between his pedaling legs.

Ciprián had already heard some rumors about how cruel she was. She was one of those girls who insisted on driving away her suitors, be it due to her whims or simply because she was convinced her father wouldn't approve. It was rumored that her last suitor wrote her a letter in which he declared his love for her. With his heart on the table, he bet all or nothing. He gave her the letter when they were alone together. She accepted it ever so gracefully and gratefully, and even opened it and read it before him. Once she was done, she looked at his eyes and smiled, held the paper filled with romantic verses to his face and tore it to a thousand pieces. What a way to break a heart!

They spent a few hours strolling around the market and the main square, fulfilling the compulsory ritual consisting of exhausting all possible conversation topics, succeeding in making good hand contact, slicing off the gap between person A and person B, before finally aspiring to go for the first touch of lips.

"I don't understand why you won't even let me give you a kiss," Ciprián said, just after failing his first attempt at her while they were sitting alone next to each other.

On that occasion, Gala had cleverly managed to dodge every single kiss possible. Trapped and watching as Ciprián's lips made their way to hers, she had to think fast. If she didn't do anything and kept her head still, Ciprián would reach her lips, the primary goal and grand prize. If she gave him either of her cheeks, the right one or the left one, he would get a meager consolation prize. If she gave him her neck, it would have been an unusual, unlikely, and unexpected move to make during the first attempt, but undoubtedly a welcomed one by Ciprián. No, Gala wasn't satisfied with any of those options, so she put her head down and bumped her forehead softly against his chest. It was a one of a kind move that left Ciprián profoundly confused and clearly unsatisfied.

"Don't be impatient. I'm not going to kiss anybody without first having strong feeling for him. For me the most important thing is to be able to have good conversation," Gala said.

"Yes, I also believe it's important to know each other well but, seriously, a kiss is no big deal," Ciprián said, grasping her by the hands.

"I feel no urge for physical intimacy. Women don't need that as much as men do," Gala said, as she took his hands and laid them to the side on the floor.

"If you wait to have all of those feelings before getting physical, what happens if you're not happy with what you get? What if you're not satisfied? Wouldn't it be better to know that the physical part will be good before you put so much time and energy into your feelings?" Ciprián said. He thought that he could convince Gala to reconsider her whole outlook on love with such deep questions.

"Maybe, but for the moment I see it my way," Gala said, standing up, and then paused for an instant. "Well, thanks for giving me a lift. I had a very nice time talking with you. I'm going home now."

"Do you want me to take you there?" Ciprián asked. He knew he had lost the battle, but what the hell?

"No. I'm fine, thank you. I'd prefer to walk alone for a bit," Gala said with a smile, and left.

I had no lust for the flesh, but evidently Ciprián did. What could I do about his sexual appetite? Nothing. I cursed the brute and beastly thing that overpowered me. It meddled with everything that was none of its business and I had no choice but to consent to it. Otherwise, it could be days, weeks, even months before I could get anything useful out of him. He spaced out, which is why I couldn't be selfish with him. There had to be a balance, a type of truce between us, in order to peacefully coexist within the same dwelling.

"I'm marrying that girl!" Ciprián said to himself, as he admired Gala's exquisite figure fading into the distance.

Shit. At that moment, I knew he wouldn't give up. He would forcefully send me off on another one of his libidinous crusades, knowing I would indulge him only to save myself from the headache of dealing with the starving and scatterbrained version of his own self. He always got his way.

Ciprián and Gala met again at a town ball. He couldn't take his eyes off her. She noticed him from afar, granted him a smile, and rushed to take another guy out to dance. Ciprián boiled in jealousy. His eyes searched for her amongst the crowd, as if they wanted to torture themselves while she laughed to whatever foolish thing that idiot said. What did that guy have that he didn't have? He couldn't understand the reason for her betrayal. After all, she was the one who approached him first, who asked him to take her out around town, who spent hours talking about silly things with him.

He finally found her alone outside, hidden among the dark landscape, contemplating perhaps the ups and downs of mountains, or the starry night, or the song of the *coquí*. It didn't matter what it was; he needed answers.

"Are you playing with me?" Ciprián said, standing behind her. She remained still. She was waiting for him. "A few days go by and you're already seeing someone else. Maybe you've been seeing him all along. You love to tease."

"Don't be silly. He's my cousin. Do you want to meet him?" Gala answered, turning around while laughing.

"It's not funny," Ciprián said, refusing to smile. "Why do you keep ignoring me, then?" he asked. He had to find out what her intentions were.

"You're the one who hasn't asked me out to dance. I have no intention of just sitting, bored to death, waiting for you to ask me," Gala said, as she got closer to him.

"I don't dance," Ciprián said.

He stared deeply into her eyes in silence. Gala did the same but she didn't hesitate; her eyes didn't even blink. Ciprián, tempted by having her standing just two inches away from him, held her waist so that she couldn't get away. He gripped her tightly and pulled her toward him until he felt her stomach rubbing his belt buckle. She didn't seem to mind his audacity. Ciprián, daring yet again to claim the rights to her mouth, finally managed to savor the juicy tenderness of her lips. His hands hastily made their way down to the domain of her fleshy buttocks, where they started to press and clench. She exhaled, slipping out a faint moan that left Ciprián dumbfounded. He clenched onto her tighter. Out of pure impulse, Gala bit his lower lip, caressing it with the tip of her tongue. Suddenly she stopped, pushed him back and slapped him in the face, making him feel the itch that came right after the burn.

"What happened?" Ciprián asked, stunned, as if he had been woken up from a deep slumber. The intensity of that moment had been battered to death.

"We're not going to do anything until we get married," Gala answered, turned away, and faded into the darkness.

Poor Ciprián lusted for her so much that he forgot how broke he was. If he was supposed to marry this girl, how would he support her? Where would they live? What kind of father would give away his daughter, coveted by so many, to a bum? He had to get answers.

His concern didn't last for long. Something unbelievable happened that week, as if there had been someone watching out for his uncontrollable sexual appetite. *El Bolipul*, the infamous underground lottery that had become his weekly vice and made him bleed out what little money he earned, suddenly gave back to him everything he had invested in it plus twenty thousand dollars.

Problem solved. It didn't take very long for him to have Gala, veiled and dressed in white, on all fours, neighing like a wild horse.

He used part of the money to buy a humble but cozy house made of cement, so that hurricanes wouldn't be able to make it fly away. With the rest of the money he purchased a warehouse, which he soon turned into a wholesale store. He called it Chepo's Cash & Carry. He began by selling domestically-grown grains, fruits, and vegetables, but he was soon in business with the capital city to bring in more canned goods.

Those days, the government was heavily investing in the economic development of the country. It was a key opportunity to begin getting people out of such high levels of poverty. Naturally, the financial backing of the United States Reserve was more than welcomed. One could see the impact of this movement year by year. As more people were able to surface from under the economic mangrove, more grocery stores flourished where there were previously none.

Chepo's Cash & Carry was the middleman those small shops desperately needed to keep growing in numbers. Their response was such that in only two years he was able to double the size of his warehouse. The expansion not only increased his capacity as a wholesale store, but also enabled him to take advantage of the growing retail market.

"Chepo, I'm noticing that more and more people stop by here to buy. Shouldn't we open up a grocery store as well?" Simón said one day at the store. Retail wasn't a new concept, but only from that day onwards did he begin to seriously consider acting on it.

"I'm not sure. For that, I would need more employees and more shelves. I'm not going to have enough room to put merchandise," Ciprián said, crossing his arms.

"Well, I think that the more people come, the better. See, I talk to business owners a bit, you know, as friends, and they tell me lots," Simón said, opening his left hand and, with the index finger of his right, jumping from one finger to the next as he listed his examples. "The prices of other stores, bad products, who has what, and who is missing what. Even then, we get hit with inventory that doesn't sell because we don't see it coming until people stop buying," Simón argued, with his eternal struggle against poor diction.

Simón had the gift of being liked by anyone he met. He liked to joke around and make friends and was a good salesman. Maybe people found him weak and harmless, and pity played a role in his favor. Regardless, the point was that he developed good relationships with his clients, not only because he genuinely got along well with them as human beings, but in addition to that, he was able to make them come back and buy more.

"So, what you're telling me is that we can get better and more up-to-date information just by speaking with housewives?" Ciprián asked.

"Exactly!" Simón answered, with a grunt that mixed laughing with exhaling. "And pricing is in our favor because we don't have to buy from any other warehouse. What do you think?" he asked, never taking his eyes off Ciprián.

It was to his advantage to move toward that direction, even as a precautionary measure. Some of those small grocery stores were threatening to become big and would soon stop buying from him, turning into direct competitors.

"When you put it that way, I'm convinced. That way we can be one step ahead of the rest. Let's try it and see what happens," Ciprián said.

The conversation was suddenly interrupted as they both watched a wrinkly old man at the other end of the store walking with turtle steps until he reached the sacks of corn. He put all the might he had left into putting one of the sacks into his cart, but his arthritis won the battle as the sack slipped from his hands. Even then, he managed to make it fall into the cart, but the hard fall made the cart slide to his side, striking another customer, a huge fat one at that.

"Fuck, can't you see I'm here?" the fat man said. He looked at the old man with threatening eyes, just like those wrestlers do on TV. Suddenly, he pushed one end of the cart into the old man's ribs, crushing his lizard body against a shelf filled with sacks of corn behind him.

If at the slightest accidental provocation he was already beating up a poor old stranger at a public establishment, I can't imagine what he would have been willing to do behind closed doors.

Ciprián rushed to the other end of the store. He almost tore off the man's shirt from his back with one hand and head-locked him with the other. He then pulled the man, trashed him against the shelf behind him, and grabbed the first thing he could reach—a can of tomato sauce—to bang the man's head until he was no longer conscious. The savage bashing left the man harmless; he would remain slow for the rest of his life.

Some days later, the old man came to the store with a proposal for Ciprián. That lizard-bodied old man turned out to be a freemason.

"We need young, capable people of good principles like yourself. We've been through too many years of politics and low resources. We have lost many brothers over the years. I believe you could help us move forward. You know, there are too many good-for-nothings on the streets," the man said, pointing his finger at one of the bruises he still had, bearing witness to the truth of his words.

As he listened to the man, thousands of ideas crossed his mind. He pictured his future brothers making Chepo's Cash & Carry the preferred vendor for both family and commercial purposes. His store would be an ideal supplier for any meeting or event for goodwill the lodge would hold. In addition to that, it would give him an excellent opportunity to network with different sectors and make new contacts, contacts who would perhaps be interested in opening big accounts with him.

"Well, thank you so much for the invitation. I'll make sure I stop by one of these days," Ciprián replied with a grin and a firm handshake.

CHAPTER V

An exemplary father

Right after getting married to Ciprián, Gala went through two consecutive pregnancies, both of them nutritionally supported by a pathologic obsession with chicken broth.

When he was two years old, Pablo, the youngest, loved to run naked around the house. Ciprián forbade it. Gala was always scolding him, but in vain because Pablo would go bare as soon as she got distracted. He would stroll around the house, carefree, enjoying the wind flowing against his privates. Every evening, upon hearing Ciprián's car as he arrived from work, he would run to his room in search of his pants. He knew what was coming if he was found pantless.

One day, Ciprián found Pablo with his pants up only to his knees. One end hung loose on the floor while the other one was beginning to tear. He was trying to put his two legs into one end, but he couldn't manage to pull up his pants. He stood still for a moment, watching his father.

"No! No! No! I'm sorry! I'm sorry!" Pablo yelled. He threw himself on the floor to take his pants off and shot out to his room, running as he cried and screamed.

"How many times have I told you not to run around with your balls hanging in the air?" Ciprián yelled at him, having managed to get him after he took off his belt. He had no mercy for him.

Irma, the eldest, was daddy's little girl. She loved to play under the house, which was raised a few feet over the ground to stop scorpions from going inside. She found a world of adventure under the house as she covered herself in mud from top to bottom. As soon as she was done exploring, the little rascal brought her muddy feet inside the house and, with a Midas touch, turned into muck everything around her.

Ciprián didn't have the heart to give her the beating she deserved. She was his little girl. Gala had to do it. The weapon of choice: an electric cable. It was thick—one of those that hang from electric posts—durable, and reliable. It left her a nice red mark that burned till the following day. Good selection to impart discipline.

Irma spent months of her childhood battling against the cable that haunted her. Gala would hide it, but she looked for it inside every drawer until she found it. As soon as she had it in her hands, she would run outside to the front of the house and throw it inside the trash can.

Gala saw it at the bottom of the trash can by chance. Naturally, she also had to throw things away every day. Irma was left incredulous as the cable reappeared to impart discipline every time. She didn't give up. She kept trying to rid herself of the cable week after week, but her mother had grown wary of her intentions. Gala kept an eye on her so that she wouldn't get her way, until one day she never saw the cable again. Many years later, Irma would tell the story of the day when she came out victorious. She went by the neighborhood's septic tank. Once there, she found a small hole and dropped the cable inside. The damned cable would spend the rest of its days drowned in shit.

Those creatures gave me and Ciprián many headaches. God knows what would have been in store for them if we hadn't corrected their bad manners!

It wasn't all tough love, by the way. He came in early in the evening and spent time playing with his children. He was a master at Parcheesi, blocking and swallowing—cruelly and with no compassion—the pawns of his naive little ones. He would laugh at the witty jokes they learned in school until he couldn't stand the pain he felt under his ribs any longer. He was amazed at how easily they could come up with tales and stories. Oh, and the questions they asked! They got more and more interesting with every year that passed.

"Dad, how do you earn money?" Irma asked during one of those nights when there was nothing to do.

"I own a warehouse with food. People buy food from me to cook," Ciprián replied.

"Oh, then from where do you get the food you sell? Why do people buy from you?" she continued her inquiry.

"Well, what I do is to buy a lot from farms or factories, so that it doesn't cost me a lot," he said, holding her by her wrists and opening up her arms as wide as he could. "Then, people come to my store and buy some of that big lot. I sell that for a bit more than what it costs me," he said, in a high pitched voice, putting her thumb and index fingers together until leaving only a hair of distance between the two. Irma couldn't stop laughing.

"Oh. But why do you sell things a bit more expensive?" Irma asked.

"Well, because they don't have enough money or they just don't need to buy as much as me. If they want to buy only in small quantities and they decide not to go to a store like mine, then they would have to pay even more. I help to make things cheaper for them," Ciprián replied.

"Do you sell the cheapest?" Irma asked.

"Well, almost. I sell almost everything cheaper, but if nobody else in the area is selling the same things as me, then I sell for a higher price." Ciprián replied, as he scratched the tip of his nose. He should have told her he sold the cheapest.

"But if you said they don't have any money, why should you sell things for a higher price?" Irma continued.

It was a very valid question to pose. It wasn't easy for everybody to put food on the table. He remembered his own father whom, when Ciprián was a child, went to the market and purchased just enough to feed his family, nothing more. From his position, he could have easily set more accessible prices so that people could get by with less.

"The thing is: I buy a lot of everything. Some things sell more than others. If something doesn't sell, I'm going to have to take the hit because I already paid for it. When I set a higher price to something, I'm pretty sure it's going to sell because people need it. There's no one else nearby selling it. That's the income that keeps me in business," Ciprián said. He wasn't sure if what he had just said made any sense.

"Uhm... I don't get it!" Irma said, after spending some seconds processing the slippery explanation that had just come from her father's mouth.

It wasn't an easy topic to explain. Those existential topics that arose from a life in business always kept me active, thinking about all sorts of issues day and night. In this case, when managing his business Ciprián looked to balance his needs, the needs of his family, and the needs of society. Whenever he ordered an additional container of goods for his store, what he was really purchasing was risk. His clients couldn't have cared less whether he was making a profit or a loss because all they wanted was to get the best price for whatever they wished to purchase. Period. If he got too greedy with prices, people would go elsewhere. If he got too stupid or too generous by setting prices too low and something unexpected happened, he could go bankrupt. Bankruptcy wouldn't have ruined just him and his family, but also his employees and their families.

There was no need to overwhelm her little girl's head with so many things to worry about.

"Alright, time to sleep! The most important thing you need to know is that daddy is working very hard so that his children can have everything they want and there's always food on the table," he said, giving her a kiss on her forehead and taking her in his arms to bed. Fortunately, it didn't take long for Irma to surrender to her sleep.

Yes, he was a good father. He made sure his family always had a good roof over their heads and food on the table. They never needed anything, a rarity at the time.

I kept in his head those same words he had said to his daughter the day before because, having just arrived at Irma's school for a talent show that evening, he noticed the dress she was supposed to wear was stained with engine oil.

43

It was his fault. He had carelessly put the dress in the trunk. He couldn't fail his girl whom, when seeing her dress, bathed herself in tears. Finding no other solution to the problem, he left the children with Gala at the school and hurried home as fast as he could to look for another dress.

Taking the twists and turns of a pitch-black road, he suddenly stumbled upon a pedestrian crossing the street, a poor bastard who was completely unaware of what was coming at him. This being one of the extremely rare occasions in which I've been able to control the body, I pushed Ciprián's foot firmly on the brake pedal a few thousands of a second before he even realized what was going on. Nevertheless, I couldn't prevent the collision.

When the car finally stopped, Ciprián remained stiff with both hands still holding the steering wheel.

"Shit, I killed him," Ciprián said.

Shit, he killed him. That's what I thought.

From across the windshield of his car, he saw a man lying on the street. Only crickets and the *coquíes* could be heard from within the pasture. He got out of his car and approached the man. He wasn't moving. He took his pulse. The man was alive but unconscious. His head was bleeding. He rushed to the trunk of his car, opened it, and grabbed the first thing he saw that could help him stop the bleeding: Irma's oil-stained white dress.

He took a look at the damage to his car. How ironic! Not even a scratch. The steel bodywork built back in the day was indestructible, unlike the plastic crap sold nowadays.

As fast as he could, he carried him in his arms and put him in the back seat of his car. Just as he rushed home before the accident happened, he now rushed to the hospital.

"Can you tell me what happened?" the doctor asked, while the man was being laid on a stretcher.

He said nothing. His mind had gone completely blank. He had no clue what to say. Amongst all the confusion and chaos, I never even considered having to answer such a simple question. I simply didn't have an answer. I'd never gone through something like that before. Neither was there, inside Ciprián's head, a memory that resembled in the slightest an appropriate reaction. I'd never even heard of anyone that had gone through something similar, nor had I ever even discussed the topic hypothetically. Nothing.

I showed him a lonely prison, a miserable life behind bars. I showed him a revolver being pointed at him. I made him feel the bullet going through his head and I made him see that same man he had just run over pulling the trigger. I showed him his wife and his children mourning his death. That was the price he would have to pay for not paying attention to the road.

"I can understand the gravity of the situation, but we need to know what happened so that we can give the patient the best and most appropriate treatment," the doctor said.

I still didn't know what to do. Showing him all the consequences of what had happened wasn't much help.

I made him revisit the events leading to the accident. At the moment it occurred, he had before himself an unconscious man lying on the street. Everything was pitch-black. The poor man most likely didn't even see it coming.

"Please sir, can you tell me what happened?" the doctor insisted.

"I don't know, doctor. I was coming back from my kid's school and I just found him lying down in the middle of the street," Ciprián finally replied and then he paused for a moment and crossed his arms. "There are so many loose scoundrels on the street; they're irresponsible," he said, gesturing his disapproval with his head.

He eluded the question, which was the most sensible thing to do. Nobody saw him. The damage had been done. Taking on any blame would have ruined the rest of his life.

Hours passed and he still hadn't left the hospital. He was waiting for news, walking restlessly around the hospital hallways and wards.

What if the man woke up and contradicted his statement? What if the man had seen him? He would recognize Ciprián because of his store. Identified by a common customer, the irony! Perhaps he saw nothing. That was the most likely possibility. The headlights of Ciprián's car would have blinded him before hitting him. But who knows what he heard? Perhaps he heard Ciprián moaning desperately as he put him in the back seat of his car, or a scream as he struck his fist over the steering wheel on the way to the hospital, or a sigh. Perhaps he had the misfortune of running over an expert in vehicle engine, brake, and wheel screeching sounds. No, that would have been too much. He probably just hit a *jíbaro* with no idea of what a car even was.

I'd had enough of this analysis. Ciprián's feet were tired from all that walking around. His eyes ached. I made him remember Gala. Many hours had gone by since he left her at the school and he hadn't gotten back in touch with her. Someone must have taken her and the kids back home, but she must have been extremely worried about him. Those days, the telephone hadn't reached the countryside so he

46

sent someone to let her know what had happened. Naturally, she would only ever get the official version of the story.

He sat in the waiting room resting his elbows on his knees and covering his face with his hands. Suddenly, one of the nurses came out of the emergency room.

"Is your name Ciprián?" the nurse asked.

"Yes. Has he woken up?" Ciprián answered. The moment of silence that followed felt like an eternity for him. The young nurse had no idea of the importance her answer would have for the rest of his life. "Did he wake up?"

"The lesion on his head caused a brain hemorrhage. I regret to inform you he has passed away," the nurse said.

Ciprián couldn't hold his tears. What a relief!

The nurse, under the impression that he was about to collapse after hearing such terrible news, covered her mouth, punishing herself for her role as the messenger.

"You shouldn't be sad! You had no control over anything that happened! You're a great man for doing what you did. You found him. You brought him here. Alive! It was God who decided to take him," the nurse said.

"Thanks. It's just that nobody deserves to die like that," Ciprián said, wiping his tears away with a handkerchief.

"Do you want to go out for a drink somewhere so we can talk? You'll feel better," the nurse said, as she caressed the palm of his hand with her thumb. "I'm Rita."

CHAPTER VI
Deaf ears
Margarita's diary: January 12, 1951

I 've already recovered from my fall, but the days keep going by and I still can't hear a thing. I was sitting with my family at the dining table the night of the accident. I remember I was distracted, nervous, and zoned-out. I had so much pressure on top of me to play at the upcoming recital, which was to be my last as a student. If everything went as planned, my teacher, who taught me everything I've learned since I was a small child, told me he could do no more for me. I would be ready to become a professional pianist. He is a great teacher and I owe him everything I know, but I think he was exaggerating. He only said that to make me feel better.

I put a lot of effort into it, but I'm not as good as the others. I can't manage to play a piece to perfection. A finger always has to get in the way and go where it's not supposed to go. A note has to play out of place or with too much pedal, cooking up a broth of notes that just ruins the melody. I get irritated because nothing ever works out my way. I would love to be able to sit down one day and let the fingers do all the work, let them make me get lost in my thoughts with the music playing in the background.

My teacher tells me that I'm very good but that I ask too much of myself. To him, nobody notices those small mistakes, not even him. My mistake, according to him, is my obsession to play a piece strictly to perfection. He says the pianist is always going to make mistakes, that those are only notes written on paper and that nobody will ever be able to play them as they were intended, not even the composer. Why? Because the language in which they have been written cannot possibly capture the level of detail or the intensity of the moment in which they were written. There will always be a part open to interpretation. It is the pianist's duty to respect the will of the composer and what he—following the storm of emotions he must have endured—was able to capture on paper at the last minute. The pianist, however, cannot forget he is human. He cannot forget to err in the name of art, to submerge himself in body and soul within the piece he plays. Otherwise, interpretation is non-existent. The pianist can only be master of his instrument when he stops playing and starts interpreting.

I hear him. I really do hear him and understand what he wants to say, but that doesn't stop me from wanting to hit the piano with a hammer every time I screw up. I disappoint myself so much that sometimes I think it's just better to leave things to those more talented than me.

I'm not the only one who thinks this way, that I'm lacking talent. None of the students hide the fact that they think I'm a big loser. They are not nice to me at all. They see me as a weakling unworthy of them. They spend all of their time gossiping behind my back. They think I don't notice them doing it, but I see them sitting on the grass giggling under the tree mocking my playing style.

I used to confront them raging mad, and they would immediately simmer down and deny it all. They would make up stories, telling me they weren't talking about anything related to me or the piano. Did I look like an idiot to them? They would come up to me while I was visibly enraged, would try to console me, and cheer me up. They would stroke my back, hug me, and caress me, having the nerve to pretend to be worried about my feelings. With such overwhelming affection, their intentions were to convince me they weren't doing exactly what I was sure they were doing. I'm not stupid. They had it against me and they still do. Now I don't speak to them. I keep walking ahead without looking at them. I don't like when people make fun of me.

It was heartbreaking to see how my own teacher also mocked me. The first thing I see when walking into the studio is him laughing out loud with the same people I'm not on speaking terms anymore. He laughs with all of them, fully aware that he's hurting me by associating with bad people that want to harm me. He jokes around and has a lot of fun with them, be it in a group or a one on one outside. I ask myself, what do they have that I don't have? Why do the lessons he gives others seem more fun while he takes mine so seriously, always going straight to the point? That's just it, isn't it? He can joke around with everyone but with me, because he can't make fun of me with me. I'm the joke.

In addition to that, during a time when I was already taking on too much stress, nightmares began taking over my sleep. My mind was blocked. I couldn't concentrate.

I'm surprised at how my brother and my dad were able to keep a straight face during dinner that day. They knew all about my dream the previous night because they were key actors in it.

It happened late at night. I was woken up by an intense light that dashed through the door and into my room. Two familiar shadows covered my bed. From the left end of the door, I recognized my brother's silhouette walking shirtless around the house, as always. At the other end there was dad, whispering something I couldn't understand despite that he had never in his life been able to lower his voice enough to whisper. I asked them what was going on, why had they turned the lights on. They didn't answer. They kept silent. I raised my voice and insisted. I had to wake up early the next day and wasn't in the mood to lose my sleep over two inconsiderate people.

They closed the door, thank God. As I managed to regain my sleep, I was again woken up by noise. It was the sound of someone stumbling against the foot of the bed. I hadn't noticed they were still in my room. I couldn't see them, but I knew they were coming closer to me from both sides of the bed. They seemed to have had it all figured out: meet in front of my room, break in from both sides so that I couldn't escape, and sneak in under the bed sheets with me.

I was terrified. I didn't know what was happening. I didn't know what they wanted from me, so I froze. I felt someone gripping my wrists together over my head. He held them firmly against the mattress with one hand while he used his other hand to stop me from screaming. He reeked of old sweat. It was dad signaling me to keep quiet. My brother, teamed up with him, took off my pajamas. I started

51

kicking but he had already grabbed me by my ankles. It all happened so fast that I didn't even get one second to react. They wasted no time. They had come to make love to me. The most disheartening thing is that I enjoyed it! I liked it! Shortly after they began, I stopped trying to get away. I gave in. I let them do with me as they wished.

After that night, dad's tender touch ceased to be what it was. Now I feel it on a different level, one that's more provocative, more sensual. I want that dream to be a recurring one. I want them to harass me and take advantage of me every night.

It wasn't real. Impossible. Nevertheless, they know what happened. I'm sure of it. They're judging me with their eyes for having conjured up, although involuntarily, such filth in my head. Even worse, they judge me because I'm still enjoying and keeping alive the false memory of being stuck between their chests.

I couldn't get what was going on with me. The things I was seeing inside my head were not right, not normal. I would have never looked at my father or my brother that way, but at that moment I couldn't help it. I knew it was madness, but madness had become my way of life. It was my new 'me'.

Luckily, mom hasn't found out about it. I don't think they've said anything to her. They must want to keep it secret. I mean, if she found out she would be devastated.

I was so distracted that I wasn't even paying attention to what I was eating. I still can still taste the bitter aftertaste from that day. There was something crunching between my teeth that wouldn't stay put. I felt both tickling and sharp scratches inside my mouth. I panicked. Food wasn't supposed to move. I had to spit out the mouthful of *piononos* so I could rid myself of whatever was inside it. My whole family just sat around the table, speechless, while my dad was right in front of me with a front row seat. His face was worth a million bucks. He not only got sprinkled by ground meat and chewed-up fried ripe plantain slices, but also half of a *pionono* smashed against his ribs.

The mess was the least of my worries. I had to know what had been hiding inside my mouth. Among the chewed bits and pieces that suddenly found themselves in flight, there it was, daintily running around my father's belly: it was a centipede.

In one quick jump, I had already landed on top of the chair. I screamed to the point where my vocal cords where just about to snap. Everyone stared quietly at me as I kept pointing to dad's belly so they could see the animal. I told them to be careful, that the centipede would bite them. My cries were ignored because, even though they had it right under their noses, they didn't see it. Idiots! They didn't believe me.

I naively believed that standing on that chair, I would be out of harm's way. I was wrong. I felt little spiky legs running from one end of my body to the other. I saw two additional centipedes: one was coming out of the collar of my blouse, making its way up from between my bosoms, and the other was coming out from under my skirt. I was certain that those venturing out were two of many more hiding under my clothes. I felt them everywhere.

I got desperate. I lost my breath. I had to get them off me. I tried unbuttoning my blouse and taking off my skirt

53

but I couldn't. My hands trembled and everything slipped. I was sweating from the tips of my fingers. I had no other choice but to tear my clothes off. Naked.

I searched my body from head to toe. As I had suspected, it was filled with those creatures. Mom ran off and came back with a blanket. She wanted to cover me up. She was saying I was making an unnecessary racket and that I needed to get down from that chair before I hurt myself. I had to make her realize that I needed help to get rid of the centipedes, not to get dressed, so I slapped her. I snatched the blanket from her hands and threw it violently on the ground. I begged for them to help me, or at least to help themselves! They stood there staring at me, waiting to get eaten by them.

The centipedes were everywhere. They kept coming and there was nothing I could do to stop them. They gathered together until they covered my feet and quickly climbed up my legs, gaining free access to stroll around the rest of my body. More and more of them made their way to me. What was going on with my family? Were they blind? Why did they insist on asking what happened to me instead of helping me get out of this nightmare?

The answers to those questions were of little importance at that moment. Besides, there was little anyone could have done against those slithery creatures invading our dining room. The floor seemed to breathe, brought to life by so many of them running around skittishly, jumping one on top of the other. They had every tile painted in dirty yellow and small black legs. They went up the walls and got tangled in my hair as they started falling from the ceiling. They saw something in me that made them make me the center of their attention. They came at me. They searched for me.

At one point I snapped. I started to cry, distressed. I felt powerless and nobody was helping me. Mom, dad, and my little brother just stood there like idiots looking at me, doing nothing to at least save themselves from being eaten alive. I was so terrified that I couldn't figure out how to get myself out of there. From where would I have gotten any willpower to help them?

I really have no idea how the hell they were able to escape from that ordeal without a scratch. This one here, the only one who did something about it, ended up in bed with an unbearable headache and painful bruises from head to toe. To me, given the imminent danger I was facing, the most sensible thing to do to get out of there was to jump out the window.

CHAPTER VII

Think about the chickens

S tanding before his most recent acquisition Ciprián—renowned as an established entrepreneur, Brother Mason, and local hero—unveiled the construction plans to what would become the newest gasoline and tire service station in town within four weeks.

The idea came as he was chatting with Simón and one of the truckers who made deliveries to his warehouse.

"You only have one gasoline station around and you have to go deep into the center of the town to get to it. To fill up my tank, I have to waste time touring the town to get there and then I have to wait in line," the trucker said.

"Can't you stop somewhere else before you get here? Or after?" Ciprián asked.

"Mr. Ciprián, I wish!" the trucker said, lifting his arms up in the air and praying to the heavens. "The thing is that if I don't make a stop here, I can swear to you that I won't have enough gas to get to the next town. Regardless of whether or not I have deliveries to make, I can't avoid having to fill up my tank here. The next gasoline station is just too far away.

"That's right, and you can see how many businesses are booming in the area. You can also see many more cars and trucks in the streets," Simón said.

"Things are only going to get worse!" the trucker said, with disapproving head-turns.

Shortly after that conversation, Ciprián purchased land in the outskirts of town, by the state road, to build his gasoline station. It would be easily accessible not only for truckers with deliveries in town or for those who just wanted to pass by, but also for the growing number of families with cars taking road trips around the island. As an added benefit, deliveries to his warehouse would get cheaper because he could offset transportation costs with the margin he made on gasoline and diesel. No way to lose!

Ciprián supervised the construction works just because he wanted to try out something new. He didn't do everything on his own, as some of his brother freemasons with good government contacts gave him a hand with getting blueprints drawn and construction permits. There was also Celín, another brother freemason, who complemented his operation by adding a *criolla* food restaurant right next to his gas station. Truckers could fill up and in the meantime, have lunch. Naturally, Ciprián supplied all of the ingredients used at his restaurant. Not too shabby.

"Chepo, tell me one thing: how come it seems so easy for you to start up a new business?" Simón asked one evening when they went out for drinks. During the time the gas station was under construction, they met every evening so he could get updates about the store.

"You remember when we used to raise chickens at home? Well, it's just like raising chickens," Ciprián said, filled with pride at the simplicity of the answer and inspired by his fourth serving of whiskey on the rocks.

"Come on, Chepo, stop fooling around" Simón said, his stutter toned down by rum, but still talking as if he had a ping pong ball inside his mouth.

"I'm being serious! See, before we started raising chickens, what was the first thing we did?" Ciprián said.

"We got the chicken coop ready so that we could fit all the chickens your dad wanted," Simón said.

"Exactly. Dad gave us wood, chicken wire, the tools, and everything else. He first taught me how to build it and then I taught you so you could help me. It was a lot of work, remember?" Ciprián said.

"I get you. But what the hell does that have to do with the gas station?" Simón said.

"Just look at the construction plans," Ciprián said. Simón took out his glasses from the front pocket of his shirt and put them on while Ciprián started drawing on a piece of paper. "It's made up of only two gas pumps: a red one and a yellow one. We're going to install them over a concrete foundation. Underground, there's going to be a gasoline tank with all the necessary piping.

"Your gasoline pumps look like two pigs," Simón said, mocking him.

"You're just jealous because you can't draw as well as me. Now, pay attention," Ciprián said.

"That other thing, what is it?" Simón asked. He didn't take his eyes off the paper. He struggled to get some meaning out of his cousin's ugly drawings. He couldn't figure out the point Ciprián was trying to make.

"Look here. Only the store is missing. I'll put the register there and have some oil and spare parts for sale. See, if you think about it: what's a store? It's four walls made out of block and cement," Ciprián said, as he drew a square on the paper. "That's it. I'm going to install huge glass windows so people outside can see what's inside," he continued, and then he left the paper in Simón's hands and drew windows in the air with both of his hands.

"What about here?" Simón said, going back to the drawing on the paper.

"Ah, that corner is for the tire shop. I'm going to set up a garage to fit one car. Does that really look any more complicated than a chicken coop?" Ciprián said.

"Well, it does to me. Do you even know how to build that? Do you know how to lay bricks and use cement?" Simón said, looking at his cousin as if he was insane.

"Well, it's not. I would dare to say that inside one's head it's easier to build a gasoline station than it is to build a chicken coop. The fact that it's bigger and made from more expensive materials doesn't mean it has to be more complicated," Ciprián said, at the same time taking his paper away from Simón's hands, folding it in half, and putting it in his pocket. "Also, I never said I was going to be the one building it. For that, I did some research and got some savvy contractors to do it."

"How do you know which design you're going to use? Do you make it up?" Simón asked.

"There's no need to reinvent the wheel because there are plenty of gas stations in San Juan. Once you can build it inside your head, the rest is easy. Things really are that simple. I don't believe anything is really much more complicated than building a chicken coop. One only needs to get the information to do it," Ciprián said.

"That's true. I can get a clear picture in my head. It's just as easy as the warehouse. It's only four walls with shelves, racks, and that's it. So, let's say you already finished building the gas station. Where are the eggs?" Simón said, buying into the idea a bit more.

"I got my *huevos* right here. Ha, ha," Ciprián said, grabbing onto his package.

"Humm, ha, ha. I thought we were talking about your big plans, not your shortcomings, brother," Simón said, holding invisible tweezers.

"Ha, ha. The eggs are the gasoline. The chicken would be the truck coming to fill up the main tank underground. While the chicken is there laying eggs and you never really know how many she will lay, the truck simply comes when you call it. You see why the gas station is really not as complicated as raising chickens?" Ciprián said.

"True. So, what would you compare the chickens to?" Simón asked.

"Don't you remember everything we had to do to care for them? It was like having our own egg factory, wasn't it?" Ciprián said.

"Yeah, I think I know what you mean. Chickens are like egg machines, right?" Simón said.

"Exactly. We needed to provide them with water, food, and straw for the machines to work properly. Machines take time to produce things, which in our case meant waiting for the chickens to lay eggs," Ciprián said.

"Yeah, we also fertilized eggs and had to wait for more chickens to hatch, and then raise them until they were big enough to lay eggs. So, that would be like buying new machines, right?" Simón said.

"Yup. For both chickens and factories, you need materials and time to manufacture and deliver," Ciprián said, sounding like a drunken professor. Simón seemed to have understood. "You need to have good planning for both, and always consider there may be delays and other risks. We're not raising chickens here; that means risks are higher now.

"But it's like you just said before, risk comes from materials and cost, more than from how difficult it may be to raise a chicken or manufacture anything," Simón said.

One could make at least some sense out of the senseless discussion between those two drunkards, especially when it came to business risks. What Ciprián was putting at risk with his entrepreneurial ventures was his family's economic stability. However, he didn't let that cloud his judgment. He could have easily determined that starting up his own business would have been too complicated, but that sort of reaction would have come from a fear of risks rather than a lack of skills. Ciprián had no fears because he understood what he wanted to do before actually doing it—oddly enough—thanks to the chickens. Understanding what he had to do gave him confidence. Confidence mitigated risks.

Ciprián would always be an entrepreneur thanks to those chickens. It was such a complete and basic childhood memory that for any situation he came across, he could easily recall it. He came out ahead as he kept figuring out how the new pieces matched with the puzzle, the big picture, and acted fast. That's how I was able to accomplish my goal of making him a wealthy man capable of supporting his family.

I know I didn't do it all on my own. I was very lucky to have Augusto as good role model for Ciprián. It's not the type of thing every father takes the time to do. Nevertheless, I felt proud of my accomplishments because I saw my counterpart in Simón who, even after he went through the same experience as Ciprián, never used that memory to Simón's benefit. Ciprián had to be the one giving him that lesson perhaps too much into Simón's adulthood to make any difference in his life.

My guess is that for Simón, that memory was less meaningful, a childhood memory left behind to give way to more important things, to adult things. In all likelihood, he never saw how simple life could have been. He must have focused on learning things that, painted in a different color, seemed to be new, but that in reality he already knew. How proud he must have felt, having gained such ample knowledge of things that were one and the same!

What would it have been like for Simón to work at the gas station? Would he have gotten all confused from having to learn something new? Would he have thought himself too old for those things? If my counterpart never made use of such a handy childhood memory, why start now?

"Well, there you go. No need for life to be so complicated. Think about the chickens, and things get a lot easier," he said, as he looked for change inside his pocket and struggled with himself to count his money. He paid for the drinks and left. Next stop: Rita's.

Drenching his cheeks between Rita's thighs, Ciprián grappled to remain anchored in place while she began to levitate from the ground. She painted curvy waves in the air, reaching out to the sky with her wide thighs. She arched her body restlessly, supporting herself firmly with her arms, intending to force the wall out of place.

"How about sticking your finger inside as you do that?" Rita had told him less than a minute before. Why didn't I think of that?

Ciprián loved to see her lose control of herself. It made him get immersed in the moment and forget the fish bouillon aroma that kept distracting him.

"I've never felt this so... intensely. Everything is new to me. I can't imagine what... comes next," Rita said, banging her head against the wall.

She knew perfectly well what she was doing. She manipulated him to her will. She knew that making him believe he was giving her the most passionate encounter of her life would make him go wild on her. Ciprián raised his head and watched her. She closed her eyes between every moan and sigh that made its way out from within.

Rita covered his eyes as soon as she noticed him watching her, shamed and defenseless, unconditionally surrendered to him. She seemed to have forgotten that she had been the one after him that night at the hospital; she had been the one who, under the influence of alcohol and seduced by the heroic feats of an impostor, brought to her bed a happily married man. Ciprián locked her wrists against the floor. He gave her no permission to be ashamed of anything. He wanted to save that instance of vulnerability for posterity, to reminisce on it during the monotonous and predictable encounters with his wife.

She pushed Ciprián back against the floor, positioning herself comfortably between his legs.

"My turn," she said. How daring!

She bobbed her head gently, twirling her tongue around him as she caressed his chest with the palm of her hand.

Upon closing his eyes, he remembered how Gala carried herself in bed, always so dependent on him, getting him to do all the work. She had no imagination, none of that spice that came so naturally to Rita, that willingness to give! While it's true that Rita could not match Gala in youth and beauty, she knew what she wanted and did what she had to do to get it. This was true not only in bed; she was an adult woman living by herself in her own house and didn't need a man to survive. The same could not be said of Gala.

Now, he also knew how to manipulate Rita, which is why he chose to make love to her on the floor. That way, even if only for a short time, he would make her be the one doing all the work. She preferred not to kneel on the floor. She didn't want to hurt her knees. In addition to that, she was distracted by the flatulent sounds that came about after going up and down among sweat, the floor, and Ciprián's back. As he opened up his eyes again, he saw her squatting over him: one-hundred percent satisfaction.

"Argh, my legs hurt. Come now. It's your turn," she said, lying down next to her lover.

Ciprián pushed her legs back until her knees reached the back of her head.

Rita twisted her head sharply from one side to the other as she gripped and pulled on Ciprián's hair. She put her hand over his mouth so that he wouldn't make noise. Perhaps she wanted to hear only herself and not be distracted. Suddenly, her breathing got more intense and she put her arms under his, chaining herself to his body. She pulled him toward her and buried her claws into his back. She let out a quivering sigh just as she let her arms fall to the floor.

Rita always stared deeply in into his eyes after making love. She didn't flinch. Her eyes penetrated his eyes, looking to bewitch him. She was so interested in him: his life, his worries, his ambitions. It was so genuine. Ciprián felt truly loved, not like Gala loved him. If only he had married her!

However, getting a divorce implied many ugly things that would come out and be placed under public scrutiny by a judge. His morals and ethics would be questioned. It definitely wouldn't have had a positive effect in his businesses or in his lodge. The only remaining option he had was to keep doing what he was doing and hide it.

"I gotta go," Ciprián said. Rita kissed him goodbye and straightened up his pants. She must have noticed he didn't have any shoes on, but decided to keep that to herself.

CHAPTER VIII
Damn jealousy

Ever since he met Rita at the hospital, Ciprián started to arrive home late. Gala, who wasn't stupid,
began getting accustomed to sitting on her rocking
chair, waiting anxiously for her husband to arrive to see with
which face he dared to look at her. Sometimes Pablo kept
her company playing on the floor until he fell asleep.

I was sure Gala spent her nighttime watch hours asking
herself: How will my husband arrive today? Will he be
drunk? Will he smell of whore? Will he be drunk and smell-
ing of whore? Clearly, arriving there sober would have been
out of the question. It wouldn't have made sense to stay out
so late if he wasn't having a good time. If he was planning to
spend his time bored, better to do so arriving early at home.

Her concerns were of little importance because, regardless of how Ciprián showed up, Gala had to keep quiet.
Whenever she began to complain, he made sure to quickly
straighten her out.

That evening, Gala didn't wait for him out on the porch.
She had to iron the clothes he would use during the week.
Ciprián arrived at around two in the morning. He walked in

a straight line, taking firm and balanced steps. He didn't wobble. He kept his posture and pretended to be sober, even when awash on whiskey on the rocks.

"Where are your shoes?" Gala said, always playing detective. That evening would be one of those where she got too nosy. Honestly, I wasn't in the mood to give her any explanations and neither was Ciprián. That's why he must have decided to ignore her and pass right by without speaking a word to her.

Gala sighed restlessly as she left some trousers mounted on the ironing board and came up to him, then began undressing him. She first took off his shirt. Ciprián, with his sight as foggy as it was, didn't realize it, but I noticed the repugnance and disgust on Gala's face after she perceived Rita's pleasant smell of roses perfuming his shirt from neck to sleeves; it barely masked the stench of alcohol emanating from her husband. The third button of his shirt from the top down: gone. She would have to spend the next day digging into the buttons she collected in a small box, finding one that matched those in his shirt, and sewing it on. She made a ball and threw it fiercely into a corner of the room, where the rest of the dirty laundry ended up.

She then took off his trousers. I doubt she would have found additional oddities there. That was the first thing he normally took off, so it was the piece of clothing with the least amount of feminine body contact. At that point, he was sitting on a stool wearing a wife-beater, white underwear, and with his black socks still on.

She now had gotten rid of the smell of roses, letting that of alcohol emanating from his mouth take over the moment, because she certainly should have noticed that Ciprián smelled of nothing else, not even his own cologne. He had taken a shower before coming back home. He knew the rosy smell would give him away. The detective wasn't dumb.

Gala went to the kitchen and came back with a bar of soap, some towels, and a bucket filled with water. She kneeled in front of him and took his socks off.

"Wearing a sock inside out, you scumbag," Gala said, furious, without realizing she was thinking out loud. Ciprián, with his ears working in slow motion, didn't even hear her. Eternally attentive to details, the detective never failed!

She began washing his feet. When she got to his pinky toe, Ciprián let out a scream of intense agony and, in a heartbeat, retired his foot from danger and sprang back his sole straight against Gala's forehead.

"Idiot! What are you doing?" Ciprián said, sweeping words out from inside his mouth. Gala looked at him as if she wanted to rip his head off, but restrained herself and said nothing. She was a patient woman. She stood up and continued ironing his clothes.

"When are you going to stop seeing that whore?" Gala shouted after minutes of silence while she folded the trousers she had just ironed. Her patience had worn thin.

Ciprián got up on his feet and grabbed her by her neck with one hand. He tightened his grip and shook her head vigorously. Gala, frightened and her face changing colors— but with the hot iron still handy—flanked him. Ciprián, in pain, let go of her neck and fled. This gave his lovely wife a chance to land another solid blow. He ended up with a triangle-shaped pink tattoo adorning his upper back.

Having wounded his pinky toe and earned himself multiple second-degree burns—while intoxicated by an exquisite mix of fermented grains—he stumbled clumsily against the stool where his feet had been washed clean like a bourgeois.

He remained there for the rest of the night. His memory had practically ceased all activity. I had nowhere to store the moment. He would wake up the next day confused and in pain, with no recollection of what had occurred.

When Gala finished ironing the four shirts and two trousers left, she put a pillow under his head, a blanket over his body, and then turned off the lights and went to sleep.

I never loved her. She simply wasn't my soul mate; let's put it that way. She had nothing in common with Ciprián. She had no education or interest in educating herself. She had no hobbies she was passionate about. She stared cluelessly at Ciprián whenever he talked business—which was his passion and what put food on the table—because it was impossible for her to follow the most basic of discussions. The only aspirations she ever had in life were to remain in the town where she was born, find a good husband, and raise her children. What could she have to teach him or their children? Was it to cook and clean?

It was like a punishment. After years idolizing his muse, he saw that from the third pregnancy onwards, little of a muse was left in Gala. Her hand-carved curves, acclaimed by many during her better years, were armor-plated by thick layers of fat and blubber laid out one on top of the other like terracotta tiles.

The harsh reality that beat him to death was that, after her beauty faded away, there was nothing to replace it. There wasn't a solid foundation of love strengthened over time. The love to which one normally aspires—that which makes you love more—was absent. He had never felt it and would never feel it for her.

It was to be expected. Her marriage to Ciprián was the outcome of a society where the act of having sex to satisfy a primitive desire of the flesh was forbidden. Of course, Ciprián got whatever he could before getting married, but he did it by paying for pieces of flesh that had taken more beatings than a *piñata* and were filthier and more used up than cleaning rags.

Unfortunately, such methods never satisfied him. Paying a woman for sex was, to him, like feeding dead game to a lion. The lion needs to hunt for his pray and kill it to be a lion. Without the thrill of the hunt, he ate, but he didn't feast. To be satisfied, he had to rid himself of whores.

During those days, however, a good and decent girl such as Gala wouldn't have gotten into a relationship without marriage. It would have been very costly for her if, due to a slip, she bore a fatherless child. She would have then ended up alone, penniless, without a husband, and no hope of ever finding a man willing to care for her and her bastard child. She would have been rejected by everyone around her. To survive, she would have had only two options: to abort or to become a whore. No, good and decent girls weren't raised to risk falling into that fate.

The two additional pregnancies Gala went through while Ciprián was seeing Rita were intense. She took advantage of each nine-month period to harass him with her jealousy, knowing that Ciprián wouldn't touch a hair on her head as long as she carried one of his kids inside her belly. Her rage intensified night after night, losing her sleep to harass and question him. She looked for clues that would prove his infidelity; she looked under his car carpets and inside the trunk; she looked for stains on his clothes and put her claws inside his trouser pockets. She searched everything as she reviled and cursed the whores she didn't know.

When she was about to have Willie, her behavior was limited to those simple acts of persecution and panic, fortunately. However, although the pregnancy with Pey began along the same lines, she somehow lost control over her mind and body.

"Every day, I was feeling as if someone was sticking a knife into my head. Then it went from attacks with knives to attacks with hammers. I couldn't sleep!" Gala said, as she closed her eyes for a moment and leaned her forehead between her hands.

"How is it that you stopped seeing?" Irma asked.

"Heck, how am I supposed to know? All I know is that everything started out foggy. I was getting dizzy, as if I was drunk. I don't know," Gala answered, not very happy with the clarity of her own answer.

"I can believe that, baby! You were like a drunk woman, banging yourself against walls!" Ciprián said comically, making everyone laugh, including Gala.

"Oh, my God! So scary!" Gala said, covering her mouth, wanting to get back to the seriousness of the topic. "Afterwards, I saw nothing at all! Pitch-black! Then I kept asking myself: Will I stay like this forever? What would be of my lovely children?" she said, and then hugged Irma and Pablo, kissing their heads. She looked lost, surely reminiscing on her period of blindness.

When I saw her saying that, it occurred to me that finding herself at risk of being permanently blind could have made her temporarily forget her jealousy. On the other hand, for Ciprián, having a blind wife also seemed to calm his antagonistic feelings toward her. That would explain the conversations they managed to have during that week, as if they had returned to their time of courtship, but would also explain the abrupt manner in which the last one ended.

"That day I gave you a ride on the bike for the first time, I had a flat tire. Didn't you notice?" Ciprián said, caressing Gala's forehead.

"No! I didn't even notice!" Gala said, in surprise.

"I had just taken it outside to see what I needed to do to fix it. I saw you were so beautiful that I couldn't risk asking you to wait while I fixed it. It would have been such a dumb move for me!" Ciprián said.

"Really? The road must have been in such a poor state that I never even noticed," Gala said, and then she paused for a moment before continuing. "You know, I never told you this, but the first thing I found attractive about you were... your teeth!" She said, giggling like a child.

Despite never loving her, their marriage was at least based on something that made them both, at a moment in life, happy. Their brief reconciliation was short-lived. As soon as she recovered her sight, she refused to believe Ciprián when he kept insisting he had been there taking care of her all week. He wasn't lying!

"I may have been blind, but not stupid. I can smell from here the perfume of that whore you've been sleeping around with," Gala said, sticking out her tongue in disgust.

CHAPTER IX

Out of this world

Margarita's diary: July 5, 1957

I 've been brought here because my parents say I'm not well, that I need doctors to start getting better. I can't see how I'll get any better. I'm surrounded by nut jobs who spend their whole day jumping, bumping against walls, and yelling nonsense in the hallways. What do they want, for me to start behaving like them? Are they thinking that bringing me here is the only way for me to get better? Do they believe I haven't been trying to get better on my own?

That's what nobody seems to understand. It was the main reason for me to leave my home. It took weeks to figure out what I should do, where to go, who could help. It wasn't an easy decision to make. I just couldn't stand her. Somehow, I had to escape from my mother's grip.

She didn't understand me. I would get yelled at for forgetting a book on a bench after reading and feeding breadcrumbs to birds, or for dropping my bracelets on the ground because they felt so heavy for my wrists, or for giving away my grandmother's watch to a friendly old man who was lost and didn't know the time. She couldn't understand that those things had no importance for me. I didn't need them to be happy; they bothered me. If something isn't important, isn't necessary, and bothers, why would I hold on to it?

Now is when I realize my actions were not the most sensible ones. Occasionally, I see the need for the things I left behind. I get mad at myself whenever I want to know what time it is and I end up having to ask others. I get mad at myself for not having as many pieces of jewelry as I did before, which I had used to make myself beautiful whenever I wanted. I get mad at myself because I won't know what will end up happening in that great book about the spiritual voyage of that Hindu fellow.

Regardless, she should have known something was wrong with me. She's my mother. She should have understood me. She should have known I had little control over my actions and I didn't really understand what I was doing. Instead of getting agitated and yelling at me, as she did so many times, she should have protected me. She should have tried to help me.

She doesn't understand what's happening inside my head. She'll never be able to understand. I don't like having her near me, someone so unconcerned with me. I hate how she looks at me, as if I were ill and there were no cure to my illness. I hate how she keeps doing spiritism and witchcraft on me. She sees me as someone who is possessed, stuck with a demon living inside me. I hate how she manages to convince dad to see me and treat me the same way she does. I hate her with all my heart for bringing me here, where I can only suffer more.

I wish she would die. I want to see her dead! That's what I told her. She was foolish enough to cry, thinking that I wouldn't notice that she was just pretending, looking to manipulate me. Great actress, she is. She always has been but I know the truth. She really cares nothing for what happens to me. She brought me here because she wanted to avoid being shamed before her family and friends. She doesn't want to help me; she wants to absolve herself of all guilt by telling everyone that I'm sick and I've stopped being myself.

That's why I spent hours and hours away from home walking the streets until late in the evening, when the racket of the day toned down and you could see from out the windows the light that flickered from TVs. I was looking for answers, an escape, an exit from it all. Sometimes I thought it was better not to come back home, to find somewhere to spend the night.

I would go house by house in search of any movement inside, any sign of life: a light on, a voice, a snore within the darkness. I wanted to find an empty house to use as hideout for the night. Night after night I failed and had to return to the home I despised. Rarely did I even get close to my goal. I would find a house that was empty and unlocked, packed with food or delicious cookies to calm my hunger. I would walk the whole house in the darkness to be sure I was alone, but I would have to run out the back door whenever the owners of the house showed up. Perhaps they noticed later on that someone had been there. I couldn't deal with my frustration, with how disillusioned I was with myself for never finding where to go. I wasn't even able to do that. I always had to return to her, confirming I was at her mercy.

Everything changed after I decided to be an independent woman. It was the perfect time to do it. My mind was clear, with none of the usual racket blocking my thinking. I wasn't hearing the wind slapping tree branches, or the heels of wealthy ladies hammering the blue-bricked roads of Old San Juan. The ruckus that cloistered me within my home that infiltrated through the walls, the floor, and ceiling, had taken a rest. The intruding voices inside my head ceased to harass me. As persistently as street sellers, they wanted me to buy into their thoughts of vice, hatred, and death.

On that glorious day, I found myself finally alone in my house, having nobody around to stop me and tell me some nonsense that would have never convinced me. I put together everything I needed to survive, the basics: skirts with blouses and enough underwear for two weeks, a pillow and a warm blanket, three or four good books to read before going to sleep, the Hanon piano scales book and some piano pieces to keep my fingers in shape, a teddy bear to keep me company, and a bunch of plantains to calm the hunger on the road.

I put all my clothes inside one of dad's old suitcases. I couldn't even close it because it was so full, so I had to take the blanket out and tie the suitcase firmly with rope. I almost couldn't carry it all. I had the plantains on one hand; with that same hand, I also grabbed one end of the blanket over my shoulder while the other end dragged on the ground. With the other hand, I carried the monster of a suitcase wrapped in rope. Minor setbacks weren't going to distract me from my goal.

Ready to face life on my own, I left behind my old home and walked around town. I was well aware that if I wanted to live on my own, I had to stop depending on my family. I wanted to have my own home, pay for my own dresses, jewelry, and luxuries. I had to pay my own dinners at fancy restaurants or buy food at a marketplace and cook for myself. In order to do that, it was vital for me to get something I'd never gotten: a job. It was priority number one.

I had no choice but to take everything with me from place to place. It was hard and pretty uncomfortable because my things were heavy, but I saw it as a good job-seeking strategy. They would see how determined I was, willing to work hard and do anything in my power to be independent, without my family's help.

I paraded by bakeries, butcher's shops, grocery shops, hotels, and restaurants. I asked enthusiastically whether they needed a young and energetic girl like me to work for them. At first, I thought I would be overwhelmed by the sheer number of attractive offers I would get and that they would fight over me. It wasn't that way at all. No one had job openings. If I learned anything from that short adventure, it was that things in this country are headed downhill. Finding a job is no easy task.

The last place I tried was a cute little restaurant with colored tiles adorning the facade. It was busy with waiters elegantly rushing to serve clients. I was all sweaty when I arrived. My arms were swollen and my back was sore from carrying around my things. The man in charge of the restaurant approached me instantly and politely. He took a *mallorca* out from one of the display cabinets and gave it to me. According to him, these had quite a reputation around town.

The first thing that crossed my mind as he kept insisting on their reputation was: to each his own. To me, *mallorcas* were just bread with powdered sugar. I had never tasted them, but as hungry as I was, I wasn't about to refuse them.

After breaking open the soft and fluffy bread, savoring it until finding myself with empty hands in the blink of an eye craving more, I knew I had underestimated them. I licked the remaining butter and sugar from my fingers, leaving no trace of what had been once simply some bread with powdered sugar.

The man who gave me the *mallorca* sat beside me while I ate and gave me a cup of coffee, which he made from a large machine with many tanks wrapped in valves and pipes. When he noticed I was looking at it, he told me it had been imported from a factory some Italians had built in Cuba. I normally don't drink coffee, so I'm not able to tell if it was any good, but the people sitting along the large counter seemed to enjoy it as they had a chat with friends.

When I finished eating, he told me with all the sincerity and empathy in the world that there were no openings at his restaurant. Nevertheless, he asked me to wait for a bit while he called up the owner and asked him if he knew of any openings somewhere else. I accepted, naturally, glad to have such an attentive person helping me and giving me hope. Besides, after the marathon I had just undergone, I took the opportunity to rest for a bit longer.

I was unlucky. The police showed up before the owner of the restaurant could give an answer to that nice man who assisted me. I was taken to the police station but I didn't make it easy for them. I kicked and screamed all the way, hoping to scare them away and that they would leave me alone just to avoid a scene.

My actions only made them more aggressive, grabbing me ever more firmly to immobilize me. Out of control and trying to force my way out, I was able to sneak out a punch that ended up breaking a window glass. The only thing that calmed my wrath against the aggressors who had me in their arms was the intensity of the pain that overwhelmed my bloody hand; my knuckles were embedded with multi-color stained glass decorations.

I already knew why they were looking for me. It had nothing to do with those false allegations from shop owners that there was a weird and confused girl walking the streets of town looking for work. Did they think I was born yesterday? Since when is it illegal to look for work? Am I strange because I'm looking for work and don't depend on a man? I know what they wanted. They knew what I had done long before arresting me and what they wanted was a confession.

Yes, I confessed to stealing the bicycle hoping they would take pity on me and release me. Why did I do it? Mine had been stolen the week before and the police, those same guys who had kidnapped me and were holding me for questioning, had done nothing to find it. What other choice did I have? It was crucial for me to get my bicycle back.

The police kept silent, surely satisfied by their easy win. Of course, I never told them why I really did it. That was none of their business. It would have been out of their ability to comprehend that having a bicycle in my hands was the only way I could see the white Martian again.

The white Martian only showed himself to me on my bicycle. He floated on top of the right end of the handlebar, following me everywhere but never communicating with me. He remained there day and night. I know because I often looked at the bicycle through a small opening on the door, trying to catch him out of place, doing something other than just elevating his sickly, wrinkly body in the air. I thought that would have given me a clue about his true intentions. He never moved from his place.

Blackness covered the whole of his pupils, vanished of any trace of what must have once been the white of his eyes. He scared me so much. I was always under the impression that he was watching my every move, studying me, searching for my weaknesses. I thought that at any moment his eyes would take me into a deep hypnosis, out of this world, with the sole purpose of consuming my soul to eradication, making my sense of self vanish.

Over time, I saw those were not his intentions. He had thousands of opportunities to harm me but he didn't. He didn't move from his place. That's when I began to think that perhaps the Martian wanted my aid, not my demise. Perhaps I was the only person in this world who could help him but he had no means to tell me what he needed. Perhaps he was counting on me to find the way.

It couldn't have been a coincidence that I was reading a book about Buddhism just when that small Martian asked for my help. It was obvious to me that I had to transcend, to reach the level of perfection of the Buddha. That way I could give good karma to the Martian, which was the only way he would have been able to live his next life as a human.

Destiny works in incomprehensible ways. Shortly after experiencing such an important revelation, such a divine quest, my bicycle got stolen. From that day on, even after stealing another bicycle just to get him to come back, I haven't seen him again. The quest became a failed crusade that got me arrested. Nevertheless, I will never be sorry for stealing that bicycle because I had noble intentions. All I wanted was to help out that little white Martian.

CHAPTER X
The voice of the people

I 'm not a stranger to hunger. I know what it feels like to be at the bottom... rock bottom... with no escape, no way out," Ciprián said, and he paused for a moment—watching seriously an applauding public—then he calmed down the crowd by raising his arm and continued his speech. "But I was raised to learn... to work... to make an effort to climb up... without looking back... Deaf ears to those who cried at me: get down from there!... You're not going to reach the top... You cannot be who you want to be!" he said, and then he made yet another pause and covered his ears with both hands, raising his elbows like an elementary school child who doesn't want to listen. "I was raised to climb up with deaf ears... until making my way out of the hole I was in... and to not only make my way out, but climb the mountain! I'm here to tell all of you who are climbing out of the hole: give me your vote! We will climb up from the bottom! Come climb with me!"

He addressed the people during the closing day of his campaign for the mayor's office of the municipality of Arecibo. Hundreds of people supported him with cries, whistles, and a frenetic applause. He had never planned to become a politician, but just one month before Election Day the mayor was still running without an opponent.

"Chepo, why don't you run for mayor?" Félix asked, at a lodge meeting. He was one of the fellow brother freemasons who helped him get the permits Ciprián needed to build his gasoline station.

"What are you talking about? Are you insane?" Ciprián said, dumbfounded by the suggestion.

"Well, why not? You're young, business is going well, and everybody knows who you are. Don't you think you could make a difference in people's lives?" Félix said, gripping his shoulder.

"You're not the only one who thinks this is a good idea, are you?" Ciprián said, referring to a few pairs of comically disguised eyes staring from the other side of the room. Félix followed Ciprián's eyes and greeted the men in the distance.

"Yeah, I won't lie to you. Some of us have already spoken about it. We think it's a good idea. You can count on our help if you run. Oh! Another thing you have in your favor is that people haven't forgotten what you did for that man who got killed in that hit and run," Félix said. Making it all the way to the mayor's office for hitting a *jíbaro*, the irony! "I think you have a real chance. You shouldn't miss it."

"Ha, ha. Well, what the hell? There's a lot to be done!" Ciprián said, raising the palm of his hand and brushing away his worries in the air.

"Everybody, listen up! See here our next mayor!" Felix shouted. As people applauded and congratulated Ciprián, Félix raised triumphantly the hand of a Ciprián who still hadn't realized what he had gotten himself into.

During his own daily struggle to climb up, he had never taken the time to look back and reflect on the development of the city. The scarcity he lived throughout his whole childhood was still a latent reality for many, forty years later. With the elections only a few weeks away, he knew that he needed to move quickly if he wanted his political presence to be felt in a city of seventy thousand people.

He went to the communities of the poor, where there were dozens of shacks with zinc alloy roofs and walls built from used-up doors, wooden panels, and used furniture. They had no access to running water or electricity, and lived there without permission. They took over uninhabitable lands covered in mangrove and dried them up, making them theirs not by the right of ownership, but by occupation.

None of those shacks could survive a hurricane. The strong winds blew away their roofs, turning them into projectiles that landed miles away to be collected and reused by another community. Torrential rains overflowed rivers and creeks, toppled hills, and uprooted large and lush trees. The waters shook the homes from their foundation and invited themselves in, ferociously and mercilessly whisking away belongings in slurry and sludge. Despite the shortcomings, people persisted in remaining there. They built stronger homes with foundations in block and cement to withstand the elements. However, they were forced to abandon them among the brushwood while they saved enough money to buy the next block.

These communities gave him a warm welcome, making his arrival an occasion. He tasted everything that came out of their kitchens, which was what they sold daily on the streets. Sweets worthy of mention: coconut candy, sesame seed candy, coconut cream candy, hard candy lollypops (*pilones*), meringues, hard cookies (*cucas*), coconut kisses, and shortbread cookies (*polvorones*). As for the fried dishes: trunkfish (*chapín*) and Ceti fish empanadas, codfish fritters (*bacalaitos*), pork rind (*chicharrones*), *alcapurrias*, and ripe plantain slices made into a ring and stuffed with minced meat (*piononos*).

These were the people responsible for keeping our country's traditions alive. For them, traditional cooking was not just a family pastime reserved for special occasions, as it had become already for those more fortunate. This was their only way to get ahead; they would be lost without it. They all wanted a better life, to leave behind the risks of hard and uncertain labor for the promise of a better live offered by the new manufacturing complexes. They all unconsciously wanted to make traditional food only a pastime. For better or worse, progress would contribute to the erosion of tradition, going from a need to a pastime, from a pastime to a tourist attraction, and from a tourist attraction to oblivion.

"We're missing the infrastructure to improve communication and commerce: roads, bridges, water and electricity lines; that way we can bring in the private sector, which is what will get us out of this standstill. Our children need to get their education but we're missing schools, especially here in the countryside. The feds have the money and San Juan controls where it will go, but it's not infinite. We're will get it, but only if we know how to ask for it. We need to be clear in what we want and how we want it. There's fierce competition among all the municipalities! Why wouldn't there be? They also want to get ahead!" Ciprián said, closing his speech. Done. Next district. We had to move fast.

Running an electoral campaign went beyond my capabilities. I helped Ciprián the best I could, keeping his entrepreneurial spirit alive. To that end, party lines were not important for me. I thought that candidates normally wanted the best for their people and truly believed they had the best solutions for problems. They would have done their best to make things better, although each in his own way. Following this train of thought, why not supply all political campaign activities for both parties with products at unbeatable prices from Chepo's Cash & Carry?

Things started off small, but with so many visits to neighborhoods, schools, government offices, police, firemen, and even the church, he was stretching his hand out to each and every public official there was. Ciprián had so much energy and charisma that supply contracts inevitably poured over him even before the election results were known.

Still, there was no celebration on Election Day.

"Chepo, you gave them quite a scare. Thirty-eight percent is huge for the party! We're going to do even better the next time," Félix said, shaking Ciprián by his shoulders.

"We'll see. Anyway, I'm not convinced with the way politics work here," Ciprián said.

"What do you mean?" Félix asked.

"That the country is divided between people who are pro-Commonwealth, pro-Statehood, and pro-Independence. That's what we call 'ideologies'," Ciprián said.

"And it makes sense, Chepo! If we don't define ourselves as a country, we won't make any progress. We've been a territory of the United States for more than seventy years, but living as second class citizens with no real representation in congress and no presidential vote. That's why we need to ask for statehood!" Félix said. It was the same old story used by everyone. Ciprián was tired of hearing it.

"Meanwhile, what happens? The *gringos* live in a country that doesn't depend on anyone else. See, they have mainly two ideologies: the Republicans and the Democrats. Correct?" Ciprián said.

"That's correct," Félix said.

"If in Puerto Rico we didn't have to worry about our status; suppose we became independent, how do you think we would organize ourselves politically?" Ciprián asked.

"No idea. Maybe it would be something like Republican or Democrat, or Socialist, or Communists. Ha, ha. Who knows! But Chepo, you know that the idea of independence isn't going anywhere," Félix said.

"Listen, listen. Now, imagine we became a state. How do you think we would organize ourselves politically?" Ciprián said.

"In that case, yes, for sure we would be Republicans and Democrats. There's no other option," Félix replied.

"Right? Now think about the people who would make up those parties. Do you think the pro-Statehood guys will become Republicans, or that the pro-Commonwealth guys will become Democrats, or that the pro-Independence... I mean, that each party would affiliate themselves in their entirety to one of the two options?" Ciprián said.

"Of course not. I would think that each person would find the party that would suit them best," Félix replied.

"Exactly! There could be pro-Commonwealth and pro-Statehood people in the same party. That's what doesn't convince me about the political organization we have today.

While we are waiting to get a non-territorial status, we're dividing all the good people we have into these parties. The same people would, in another life, be together by their ideology, by the ideals that last regardless of which status we have as a country; they wouldn't be grouped by status," Ciprián said.

"That makes sense. They're always stepping onto each other's toes not because an idea is bad, but because they both want to take credit for it," Félix said.

"Right. It makes no sense for us to be organized the way we are because defining our status doesn't guide us to the best way to tackle poverty, education, or crime. Status is important, but we're splitting up good people rather than using them to come up with better solutions for our big day to day problems," Ciprián said.

"I see. Just as, no matter who wins the elections, all the parties are going to be asking for the same federal funds. The winning party will get to think about how to invest them, disregarding other parties as much as it can. We're voting to see who can manage funds better," Félix said, and paused. "But what would you do then?"

"I would turn everything upside down. People should cut ties with political parties based on status, make them a second priority, which is what true ideologies are at the moment. They should put true ideologies as a first priority. That's it!" Ciprián said, wiping his hands clean of the issue.

"I wouldn't want to take a stab at it," Félix reacted.

"Sadly, neither would I. Only God knows if by just speaking about this we'll get ourselves killed and thrown in a ditch. Ha, ha, ha," Ciprián said.

The next day, Ciprián and Félix met again in the lodge. Ciprián had never seen Félix with such a somber face.

"Chepo, I say goodbye, my friend," Félix said, taking him by the hand and gripping it firmly.

"Why so serious? Where are you off to?" Ciprián asked.

"You see, my wife and I have been thinking about moving to New York for a while now. We made the decision today. You know things aren't going well here and the kids are getting big. We have to look for a better life!" Félix said.

"I never would have guessed it. You never told me! Do you know what you'll be doing there?" Ciprián asked.

"Well, some other relatives have moved there and they say there's a lot of work. There are many Puerto Ricans, too. You know I always find a way to make it. Ha, ha," Félix said, hoping Ciprián wouldn't notice the mask he was wearing. The expressions of his eyes and his smile lasted too long for what was considered normal or genuine, falsely covering up his insecurity. A new job, a new city, a new country, such an adventure! It could just as likely be a living hell without a steady income and a wife and children to support.

"Hey, why don't you get some Corvettes over there and send them here so I can sell them?" Ciprián said. He wanted Félix to start off well his new life. At least, he would move in the right direction. Besides, I had already prepared Ciprián's head to build a car dealership next to his service station.

"Another business? What are you going to do with so many businesses, Chepo?" Félix said with his mouth still wide open.

"Well, here's how I see it: if people buy a car, what will it run on?" Ciprián said.

"Gasoline," Félix said.

89

"Come get it!" Ciprián said, like a cheap ad announcer.

"Then, the same John Doe who bought the car has to eat, right?" Ciprián asked, keeping the same comical tone.

"Come get it!" Félix said, imitating him.

"I get 'em, regardless!" Ciprián said proudly.

"Ha, ha. Well, I don't know. If I were you, I'd grow the businesses you already have," Félix warned.

"Grow them how?" Ciprián asked. Thanks to the elections, he had just signed a one year agreement to supply all public school cafeterias with food and another one to be the preferred gasoline supplier for the fleet of old Harley Davidson motorcycles and Volkswagen Beetle police cars. He was also undergoing negotiations for two additional contracts, which would supply town fairs and Christmas, New Year's, and King's Day celebrations.

"Set up more gas stations and warehouses. You're making money out of them, right?" Félix asked. Absolutely.

"Yeah, they're doing alright, but I'll leave the growing to the big guys who know more than me and have more money than me," Ciprián said, in a humble tone.

"Man, you have the whole island at your disposal!" Félix said, patting him on the back as if he was making him see all the opportunities he was missing out on.

"True, but soon the big guys from San Juan or from abroad will make their way here and take everything," Ciprián said. Another reason was that he just didn't find it a challenging idea. Simply repeating the same business model in other places was boring to him. It was boring for me too. We liked the hard part, where setting the first stone was difficult and risky. We wanted to try out new things and take advantage of opportunities others were missing out on. We couldn't stay still doing the same thing. Naturally, he wouldn't tell his friend, bankrupt and forced out of the country, about his petty personal desires.

"That's true. I can bear witness! Well, you've always been able to get your way by using your smarts more than me, and things have always turned out well for you. I can't be a critic," Félix said.

"So, what do you say? Will you get some cars for me? I'm sure that just to indulge themselves, people will get the money from where there is none," Ciprián said.

"Why not? Give me a few weeks while I get settled and I'll get back to you!" Félix said, feeling more content.

Within two months of Félix moving to New York, Ciprián got a call from the port to pick up the four containers he had just received. Inside, he found brand new, 1960 Corvettes painted white, red, blue, and black. They would stock the new showroom he built next to the gas station.

The first thing he did was to take his family out for a ride. Since he only had one passenger seat, he had to make four trips, but he hung a sign on each car that said, "You want it? It's yours!" He would go around the whole town and spread the word.

He took Gala out for a ride first. For her, he chose the white Corvette. He saw it as a symbol to the artificial purity of their marriage.

"I like it this color, in white, so that it doesn't absorb so much heat from the sun," Gala said. How practical! I found white extremely dull.

"What does that even matter? The top is up and we're only going to be out for a few minutes," Ciprián said.

"It feels fresher, in my opinion," Gala said. Women!

He took her around the surrounding neighborhoods—those close to the house—letting her wave like a princess at people coming out into the streets, attracted by the engine's rabid growl. They all saw him parading his wife, all happy and smiley. Perhaps that could have been a way to stop gossip and ill-intentioned rumors.

When he came back, he got ready for the second round. Since Pablo was the eldest son, he picked him up in the sexy red Corvette and took him to the neighborhood around his warehouse. Ciprián didn't want only his potential clients to see it, but also wanted to show it off to Simón.

"It's really nice, Chepo. You're going to get me this one for my birthday, right?" Simón said. He pointed at Pablo with his lips while looking at Ciprián. His son was standing in front of the Corvette, hypnotized.

"You just wait for it. What are you going to give me?" Ciprián replied.

"My thanks," Simón said, and laughed. He kept looking at Pablo, who strolled delicately his hands over the bodywork's soft and elegant curves. "Be careful, kid. You'll fall in love! You like it?"

"It's cool!" Pablo replied, fixated on the car.

He picked up Irma in the blue Corvette. She seemed to have no interest in the machine, but wanted to enjoy the breeze and take on fresh air. He took her around the town square, a very busy place during the weekends, and they sat on a bench to drink raspberry snow cones (*piraguas*).

"Dad, why did you stop loving mom?" Irma asked with a tone of innocence. That's what he got for spending time with his children.

"One second, honey. I think that man wants to ask about the Corvette," Ciprián said, quickly slipping out of the car. His daughter must have gotten upset, but at least she didn't bring up the topic again on the way back home. She would get over it.

Finally, he picked up Willie and Pey in the black Corvette. They were still small, so they fit together in the same seat. He gave them a ride around Rita's neighborhood.

CHAPTER XI

Gala's holidays

C iprián's two youngest children were the only ones who knew where Rita lived. Ciprián took them there so that Gala wouldn't get suspicious. Who would think that a cheating husband would take his children to his mistress' home? This time, he arrived with them in the black Corvette.

The kids played in the backyard while Ciprián and Rita locked themselves in. They had more than enough to stay entertained: looking for hidden treasure among the plants in the yard; making houses with stones, given the yard was composed of ninety percent bits of tile and ten percent earth; catching lizards with leashes made from grass.

"What will you do with her?" Rita asked Ciprián. They had just made love and now this. First Irma and now Rita? He was taken by surprise and had no escape. He knew this question would come but he wasn't ready to answer it.

"Why are you asking me this all of a sudden?" Ciprián answered. He was fed up. He turned around on the bed with his back toward Rita. He didn't want her to see his eyes while he tried to come up with a lie.

"I don't know. Just to know," Rita said, remaining calm. She touched his body with hers and caressed his arm up to his shoulder.

"You know it's not an easy decision to make," Ciprián said. His reputation, his business, his children, his wife's miserable future... many things on the line! But he felt so good by her side!

"You're exaggerating things!" Rita said. She both combed and messed up his hair with the tips of her fingers. He lay still where he was.

"I don't know what to do. I'm going crazy," Ciprián said, sighing. Why did she have to ruin his day?

"It's not so difficult. Which one makes you the happiest?" Rita said.

"Please, don't make me choose now," Ciprián begged her. Of course it was her! At the very least, he would be better off with her than with Gala. If he didn't have a wife and children, he wouldn't have thought about it twice!

"Silly! If I were you, I would keep the Corvette just for fun. It's cute," Rita said, dismissing Ciprián's preoccupations. The Corvette! The knot he had on his heart was immediately unloosened. For this topic, he was ready.

"You make a good point, but I'm not sure, I think I'll keep the Bel Air. It's old but it runs well," Ciprián said. The Bel Air was a pretty common car, convenient if he had to take Rita out for a ride. He both could have and wanted to keep the Corvette, but it was too flashy.

"When are you taking me out in it?" Rita asked.

"It'll have to be some other day, dear. They're already sold. I have to deliver them this afternoon," Ciprián said. Risk being seen with her in the Corvette? Never!

He not only brought his children to his mistress' home, but also made them eat there. Rita insisted on it. However, she looked nervous all the time, insecure around them. She wanted to leave a good impression on them, to win them over, but was not confident that she was getting there. She had no children. Perhaps her lack of experience made her uncomfortable. Perhaps her conscience worked against her, making her perceive resentment from them for being a home-wrecker. Were they old enough to know what was really going on? Could they be thinking his father was just visiting a friend?

The *alcapurrias* Rita cooked were the only thing that seemed to break the silence on the table. One could only hear the subtle crunching of teeth going past the tannia and plantain crust, ceasing as soon as the filling was exposed.

"Are they good? Do you want me to fry more? Or, would you like more rice with sausages?" Rita asked the children, while she molded the *alcapurrias* into a potato shape before frying them on the pan.

"I'd like some more but why do they taste different?" Pey said.

"What do you mean, different? They're made from crabs. Didn't you ever try them before?" Rita asked.

"No. Mom always puts meat on them. She doesn't like crab," Willie said.

If there was any resentment toward Rita, it wasn't evident. On one hand, it could have been because they couldn't figure out what was going on; on the other hand, perhaps they didn't say anything out of the fear of being beaten by their father for misbehaving. Nevertheless, the instructions Ciprián gave them were crystal clear.

"When we get home, you're going to eat everything Gala cooks for you!" Ciprián said, turning toward them over the driver's seat. "And God help you if you tell her you've already had something to eat! And don't say a word about Rita! Is that clear?" he warned, pointing his finger at them.

Gala's well-founded jealousy and suspicions were progressively escalating to new levels of tension within the marriage. Ciprián noticed how all of his things were now being searched daily. He endured never-ending confrontations and questioning: What did you do? Why did you do it? Who were you with? Where were you? How long were you there?

Naturally, she had every reason to delve into his business. Her husband was being unfaithful to her and shamelessly denied any wrongdoing. He mocked her.

"Dad! You have to come home! Something is happening with mom. She's going crazy! I don't understand!" Irma said over the phone, calling to his office on a Saturday at noon.

"Sweetie, calm down. What's going on?" Ciprián said.

"She's just skipping and jumping around! I'm trying to get her to calm down but she doesn't listen or say anything to me! She's only blurting out a lot of nonsense! You need to come and see! I don't know what else to do! I need help!" Irma said, while she moaned.

"Cuuunt! Fuuuck! Shiiit!" Gala screamed, scraping her throat. He could clearly hear his wife yelling through the receiver. She quickly went from one profanity to the next, at times combining the filthiest swear words her head could come up with, elongating a syllable of her choosing for at least five seconds and raising her decibels each second she sustained it. They came out of her mouth with such fluency!

"On my way," Ciprián said. He thought it was another one of her stupid jealousy tantrums taken to another level, but he wasn't ready for what he would find. He imagined her as usual, tense and red as a tomato, at the verge of exploding. He knew well the ritual she followed to unleash her fury. However, she was out of place by becoming a pest and causing a scandal around the neighborhood. A good beating would get her to shut up.

That's what he was intending to do as soon as he arrived to the house but he didn't hear screaming coming from inside anymore. In the living room, one of the armchairs had tilted to its side and rested over the coffee table, which evidently had been pressed past its breaking point given his wife's unearthly weight. The resulting seism must have shaken all the picture frames to the point of dropping from the walls; it must have catapulted the porcelain figurines to their death, smashing them into a thousand pieces and scattering them around the floor. There were papers everywhere. The curtains were out of place, torn into bits and pieces as if by a savage beast.

"Irma!" Ciprián shouted in whisper, upon hearing the whimpers coming from her room. Seeing the mess around, he didn't want to alert Gala of his presence. Only God knew how she would react if she saw him. Irma unlocked the door to her room and opened it.

"She's in the kitchen" Irma said. She pointed to it from inside her room just by the door, wiping her tears away from her eyes.

Water flowed freely, filling up the sink and cascading into a spring of rice leftovers, beans, vegetables, and meat fat that extended to the entirety of the kitchen. Water was slowly making its ways toward the living room, swamping Ciprián's shoes as he got closer.

The stove burned to the max, but only one of the burners was busy; it kept on heating a pan with boiling oil, which crackled on its surface. From within, big pieces of what appeared to be green plantains fried to the point of turning into coal were spit out violently.

At last, he found Gala. She was sitting on the puddle, cutting pieces of meat on the floor while humming some song he didn't recognize. She was wearing a nightgown with flowers. Her legs were wide open but she was not wearing any underwear. The leftovers from the kitchen sink were amassing between her thighs.

"Hi," Gala said. She seemed to have calmed down. She smiled at him with her eyes, like she did before their marriage. She had just finished cutting another slice of meat. She put it to her side at the top of a mountain made up of a hundred others. "Chepo, it will be time to eat soon. Dinner's almost ready."

Ciprián was left speechless. It gave him goosebumps seeing her in that state, so close to him with a knife in her hand. He returned the smile before making his way back into the living room; he didn't want to disturb her. He grabbed the phone and made a call.

Gala, evidently losing her self-control, had to be interned in a mental hospital at the capital city. She did put up a fight, however, gunning down with slices of beef the men in white who abruptly came into her house to take her. She tried to flee, but running barefoot over a puddle of water, her surroundings didn't work to her advantage. She slid and fell on her ass, bluntly and with force.

Ciprián had his parents stay at his home for a few days. He wanted to restore in his children some sense of order, sanity, and peace after the chaos they had been through. Although she would never miss such an opportunity to spend time with her grandchildren, Flora set some conditions before accepting the deal.

"If you want me to help you with your kids, then I want you to come straight back here from work," Flora said. His mother would make sure order was enforced not only to the children's daily life, but also to Ciprián's.

"Mom, I'll do whatever you ask. You're the boss here!" Ciprián said, giving her a big bear hug.

"Don't you 'mom' me! No drinking, no mistresses. I'm not dumb! You're not going to send me to any nut house! I'm too old for those things!" Flora said, as she pushed Ciprián away, and then smacked his face.

"Ouch!" Augusto said, from behind his wife, pretending to play a *güiro* with his fingers and forearm to tease him.

"You're not allowed to get funny either, mister! He must have learned to behave like this from someone!" Flora said.

Having his parents at home was like reconditioning his behavior and thinking. It was as if at the time he turned into an adult and left home, not only his memories, but the way he behaved toward them, had been stored in a corner to be reactivated only in their presence. He followed instructions, was polite, wasn't violent, and didn't drink. In short, he avoided doing anything that could cause a bad impression. He had such respect for them that if he used a swear word by accident, he feared being scolded and would get shivers up his neck just like it happened during his childhood.

For the first time since he met Rita, he arrived home early every day. The kids around the neighborhood, who always took advantage of his absence to spend the afternoons glued to his TV, were perplexed at the transformation they saw in Ciprián when his parents were around. They had been scared away like street dogs thousands of times before, but that week they weren't. They had Flora and Augusto to thank who, grandparents after all, loved to be surrounded by children. Although he didn't openly show it, Ciprián also felt relieved to take some days off from everything complicating his life, especially when Augusto showed up with guava pastries. Delicious memories!

Ciprián's childhood had this curious effect on the relationship with his parents after he became an adult. I asked myself, what would the future have in store for him after putting his efforts into supporting his family and being a good father to his children?

Since her return from the mental hospital, Gala seemed to care little for her husband coming back home late. They did something to her there that left her docile, with no intention of throwing any more tantrums related to affairs and mistresses. She still had sleepless nights though, this time because she was worried about her daughter who, many times per week, was suddenly awakened by severe panic attacks.

I couldn't imagine how terrifying it must have been to wake up from a deep slumber and feel tied to the deepest end of a pool, struggling to get oxygen into her lungs, with her heart insisting on drilling through her chest and make an escape. I couldn't pretend to understand what it would have been like for her to live with the constant fear of not knowing if she would wake up the next day bathed in sweat with a rope tied around her neck wanting to take her hastily into the next world.

Gala sat with her on the bed every night, and tried to calm her down as she lived her nightmare. She gave her water to drink, stroked her, and lowered her temperature with a cloth soaked in cold water; she couldn't do much else.

One night, having just calmed her down from one of her attacks, Ciprián came in drunk on whiskey, slamming on doors without saying a word. He got to his wardrobe and took out a yellow cigar box he had hidden at the top. His children had never seen that box before.

"What's going on?" Gala said from Irma's room.

Inside the box there was a cigar, two bullets, and a short barreled revolver wrapped in cloth. He took the revolver out and walked up to Pablo's room. The door thundered against the wall, making his son jump from his bed and ending up on all fours like a cat in alert.

"You stole twenty dollars from the warehouse, didn't you, you little weasel?" Ciprián said. He pointed the gun at his head and rested the tip of the gun barrel on his forehead.

"No, I didn't take anything! I swear to God!" Pablo answered, trying to get away from the revolver as he cried. Ciprián followed his movements with the gun barrel still pressed on his forehead, pushing harder the more his son moved until he was trapped between the gun and the bed's head board.

"Do you think I'm stupid? All of these years as the owner and not once has anyone stolen from me! Some piece of shit like you had to come, my own son, and steal from his father!" Ciprián shouted. He wanted to teach him a lesson.

"Stop, please! Look at what you're doing to him!" Gala said. Neither Gala nor Irma dared to come into the room. Pey and Willie held them by their legs. They were frightened. They didn't know what was going on.

"Dad, please! I didn't do anything! I was only playing in the warehouse!" Pablo said. He had a knot in his throat that almost didn't let him breathe.

Without taking his eyes away from his son, he quickly raised his gun and shot at the wall leading to Willie and Pey's room, causing shrieks of terror.

"Tell me it was you who took those twenty dollars!" Ciprián shouted, pressing the hot gun barrel on his forehead.

His son had four Lincoln bills hidden under a mountain of underwear inside one of his drawers. Ciprián boiled with rage. He was hoping that somehow he wouldn't need to witness his son's confession. He had put so much effort into giving them all a great life only to be repaid by them with lies and treachery.

"You... weren't... taught... to steal!" Ciprián said, as he beat his son furiously.

However, his erratic behavior rooted not from alcohol or his son's treachery, but for the scandalous news Rita had given him that same evening.

"I'm pregnant," she said. That phrase still echoed loudly in his ear. He had to release his anger somehow.

CHAPTER XII
An irresistible body
Margarita's diary: February 18, 1960

I despise Gala. She thinks I'm naive, that I'll just believe whatever happens to come out of her mouth. Just today, she had the nerve to tell me that Luis had committed suicide yesterday. She told me I had been found in his room sleeping next to him with my entire body soaked in his blood. She even came up with this story of how all his shit had to be cleaned off my chest.

Obviously, that never happened. I told her to stop behaving like a child, that it wasn't the type of things people should joke about. She didn't stop. She thought herself funny by putting up her skeptical face. She kept harassing me, asking me questions about how could it have been possible that I remembered nothing if I had been there with him when it happened. I may be in a mental hospital but I'm not crazy. Gala thinks that just because I'm here, that automatically makes me a complete idiot.

Yes, I woke up with a hangover. I was dizzy and couldn't stand the headache. I have Gala to thank for that given we drank so much of that rum the night before. Yes, when I woke up I was there curled up with him. The nursing staff came knocking down doors as always, with such little regard for their patients. They carried me out of the room in an instant. They were in such a rush to bathe me that they didn't even let me say goodbye to him!

The bath brought me relief. After all the sweating last night, my skin felt sticky. However, I feel pity for the nursing staff. They're short on people. They want to cover the whole ward with only three people when, in reality, they need ten. They have them running up and down like worker ants because they're in constant emergency mode. They were so overwhelmed by the workload that they didn't even say anything after they found out I had spent the night with Luis. I was sure they would have thrown me into the dark room.

I haven't seen either of them, neither Luis nor Gala. There's no doubt in my mind that she took him from me. That's why she tried to fool me. And how! They ran away together. She always said he was handsome. She turned the whole nursing staff against me. I asked them about Luis and they told me he was discharged, that I won't see him again. I asked them about Gala and they told me she was also discharged, as if she was in better mental health than me! Everybody I'm supposed to trust wants to take advantage of me. How dare they? How can they look at me in the eyes and mock me?

But what a night! One of the guys from the nursing staff had his eyes set on Gala so he got us a bottle of rum. We drank so much! It gave us a good chance to get to know each other better.

She has kids and a husband living in Arecibo, but according to her, the husband is a womanizer. He leaves the house early in the morning and comes back late at night drunk and scented by women. The neighbors, with their innuendos that point to their marriage falling apart, are already telling her she should be looking for potential replacements in case she ends up alone. They're made aware of his adventures well before her.

Even at school, her kid's classmates know all the gossip. I know how cruel they can be. They're willing to put ideas into her kid's heads just for a laugh. Little do they care of how much they make them suffer. The oldest one, her girl, came home crying one day. The gossip of the day was that her father had gotten divorce papers so that he could marry his mistress.

The damage being done, it was Gala who had to manage the crisis. She has to keep her composure even if she's dying inside. What to say to your child when she asks you if her father has his divorce papers ready? Shouldn't she have been made aware of what was coming before her children were?

Her husband has the two youngest ones on his side. They support him by covering up his bad deeds. They know everything their father has done but they turn mute as soon as Gala starts questioning them. She says that they don't love her, that they don't see her as good mother and would rather replace her. I think she's exaggerating. I don't think it's possible that such a good woman could be hated by her children. If anything, they're confused. Perhaps they don't know what they're doing.

I can't understand how anyone could stay with a man like that, a man so demeaning who makes her feel less of a woman than what she really is. In my opinion, she still loves him blindly even if the opposite seems more likely. Her eyes sparkled when she told me how he was when they got married, how he used to lay her in bed and kissed her madly, how he kept whispering "I love you" into her ear. She never got tired of it. Those words are so beautiful and have so much meaning!

He must have done something to keep her stuck in that emotional blindness. Could he have put a spell on her? Could he have truly loved her at the beginning of their relationship? Could he have wanted to make sure she would stay madly in love with him forever? It seemed like the perfect example of a spell cast in good faith by a lover, but one that ended up kicking him right back in the ass for being so selfish. That must have been what put her in that state. Her husband thinks only about himself and doesn't have the dignity to revert the spell that has left her so stupid.

Gala doesn't believe in witchcraft. The way she sees it, he doesn't have the balls to stand in front of her and tell her "I don't love you anymore". According to her, that would be enough for her to move on. Although I do believe she's convinced this is what she needs, I also believe that if he tells her those words exactly as she's asking, her whole world would crumble. Those are very strong words to hear. If her husband is heartless enough to tell her that in such a direct manner, then he deserves that the devil resurges from hell and swallows him whole.

All I told her was to take a good look at her husband's actions. She has to hold her hand over her heart and ask herself: cheating or not cheating, did she still love him? If she did and she wasn't willing to leave him, then she had to accept him for who he was and all the faults that came with the package. She's harming only herself with all that jealousy.

She's the one living inside a mental hospital, not him or any of her children.

She keeps insisting that I don't understand what's happening, that I won't be able to understand what she's going through until I get married. As a wife, there is a sense of pride that can't be ignored, she says. To that I say that pride is worth nothing if it brings misery instead of happiness.

After a somewhat uncomfortable silence, she seemed to cheer up again when I began telling her about Luis, about the day when we had met during the previous month.

Luis and I were alone together watching TV. I felt like a goddess. The TV ads were showing me all the things I needed to see. The most famous TV stars, Helena Montalbán and Braulio Castillo, would get out of character and start to talk about me. They knew what I was doing, what dress I had on, how I felt, when I laughed or cried. They gave me love advice and cared so much about me. They adored me!

That helped get enough courage to talk to Luis. He was so handsome, like the ones who stared at me from the TV set. He had a way about him that made him do anything and know everything. He was a god and I was a goddess. We were destined to be together. However, with all the nice things I said about him, it was unavoidable that Gala would ask me how such a wonderful guy could ever end up here.

They put him in here because he had many issues at home. He told me how horrible and strict his mother was. She treated him like a child. He almost had to ask her for permission to breathe. He wasted his days attempting to escape from her dictatorial shadow, which observed his every movement, criticized his every mistake, and gave him orders.

One day, he just couldn't stand her anymore. He had to get out but he couldn't figure out where to go, but he was sure that any other place would be better even if that meant going to heaven ahead of time. That's when he showed me the knife scars he had on his arms. He let me caress them, and feel the tenderness and roughness of his skin. I felt so comfortable around him. We connected instantly.

When we got to that part Gala interrupted me. This is when it all began. She was the one inciting me to go get him. I owe such an unforgettable night to her, my angel. She held me by my shoulders and began shaking me to make realize what a heartthrob he was, as if I needed convincing! She yelled at me, telling me I had to go to wherever he was and show him how much I wanted him. I hesitated. I got so shy. What if he rejected me? I would have felt so embarrassed!

At that point, the guy who had brought us the bottle of rum came back. He said some things to Gala's ear that made her giggle a lot. He was a very friendly man. While Gala kept chatting with him, I stood by the door thinking, struggling to make a decision. Should I stay of should I go? If Gala hadn't kicked me so hard that I ended up outside in the hallway, I probably wouldn't have gone. However, the last thing she told me finally convinced me. If Luis was half the man I was telling her he was, he wouldn't be able to resist spending the night with me; he wouldn't reject me.

I locked myself in his room. I left the light off so that he wouldn't wake up until I surprised him. I took my clothes off, dropped them on the floor, and snuggled carefully with him. Luckily, he didn't wake up. I wanted to catch him by surprise and snatch him from his slumber. I wanted him, upon opening his eyes, to feel my head between his legs and give in to me just as Gala said it would happen. It took some effort, but I managed to get him to lie on his hips until I was able to reach him comfortably. As soon as he let go the subtlest grunt, I knew he wouldn't be able to say no to me.

Luis kept quiet and didn't move at all. He still pretended to be in a deep sleep so that he could get all the attention without having to return the favor. I played into his games. I wanted our first night to be unforgettable for him. I wanted to do all I could to satisfy him, to treat him like a king. I slid my body against his and wrapped him between my legs.

I can't remember the rest. He must think I'm so stupid for falling asleep before finishing what I started. I'll never get another chance to do it right. That must have been the reason why he ran away with Gala. She's definitely a better woman than I am.

CHAPTER XIII

Unforeseen collision

Although still dizzied by a hard blow to her forehead and with her arm covered in bruises, Rita came out of her car as soon as she could to give first aid to the injured woman. She was still conscious but blabbing nonsense, so it became impossible to figure out what she wanted. Rita had no choice but to try to keep her awake and alert. The front end of her car had compressed into itself like an accordion, totaled, leaving her stuck between the steering wheel and the front seat with loose pieces of metal puncturing her stomach. She was bleeding from her belly and breathed anxiously. She couldn't move from her place. Rita didn't dare to touch her.

At a crossing, the woman kept going straight until crashing into Ciprián's car. She struck him somewhere around the front wheel of his car, making it turn ninety degrees. Despite some scratches and Rita's bruise, they came out of the accident unharmed. Ciprián, accustomed to having a certain degree of alcohol running through his veins, had taken the wheel as usual. They were heading back from a gathering hosted by Rita's inconceivably dull family.

The woman behind the wheel was not as fortunate. She crashed head on, which made her fly head first over the wheel and into the glass, where it left a star-shaped cranny that kept growing in size until taking over the entire surface of the window pane.

It didn't take long before people from around the neighborhood started showing up. They bundled up around the crash, curious to know what had happened. Ciprián, apart from the accident, had another situation to worry about. He was unfortunate enough to have a car crash in broad daylight—with his mistress and illegitimate son—just by the neighborhood in which he lived with his wife. Only a few blocks away from his home, those surrounding him were his next door neighbors.

In addition to that, someone came up with the fabulous idea of alerting Gala, who quickly showed up to the site of the accident. This was the first time she saw Rita and Quique, but she recognized them immediately, as if she had their faces painted in her head thanks to the one million brush-strokes that rumors and stories painted on her imagination. She wasn't shocked by what she already knew. She approached the site confident, serious, composed.

"You're nothing but a filthy whore," Gala said to Rita. Gala then turned to Quique, who still rested on Ciprián's arms. She seemed to be looking for his father's resemblance. She must have noticed he had his eyes and forehead. On the other hand, his mouth and stretched cheeks belonged to his mother. She took a few moments to observe the repugnant hodgepodge with disgust. The poor kid, at five years old and having just experienced a frightening car accident, had no idea of what was going on. He didn't know who was that loud-mouthed, obese woman cursing him with her eyes and making his mother cry.

"Gala—" Ciprián said. I don't know what he was going to say, but he was interrupted by his wife.

"You're nothing but a mouse," Gala said to Quique.

She said nothing more. The silent multitude made way for her as she turned back and went back home.

Before Ciprián could react to such a disastrous event, both the ambulance and the police had arrived. Thanks to two or three eye witnesses, the police were able to corroborate Ciprián's story for their report while the ambulance took care of the injured woman.

"Chepo crossed a yellow light, and it seems this woman didn't see him coming. Sometimes women think they can just cross red lights without paying attention to other cars. They just don't know how to drive," attested the witnesses.

The two police officers, who knew Ciprián well since the last elections in which he ran for mayor, omitted the state of inebriation on their report.

Days later, Rita would return to the hospital with news about the injured woman.

"Chepo, that girl who crashed into us died yesterday night. Poor thing. May god bless her!" Rita said.

When the accident took place, Rita had been busy reading a fashion magazine. She never knew that Ciprián had crossed the red light.

It wasn't easy to convince Ciprián to be faithful to Gala, whom he didn't love. Likewise, it wasn't easy for me to convince him of leaving her, disgracing her and his children. It wasn't easy for me to convince him to leave Rita, his tempo-

113

rary relief, nor drinking, which made the whole ride more pleasant. What was easy for me to convince him to do was to forget accidents. Did he feel guilt? Honestly, of course yes! It would be inhuman not to feel any remorse or guilt after having experienced something so terrible. Nevertheless, my job was to keep him strong and make him see what was at stake.

As I implanted it in his head—having analyzed the situation—it was just an accident. Both drivers were on the road not paying attention to one another. Yes, it's true that Ciprián had been drinking, which would explain why he crossed the red light, but who can tell me that at the moment of impact Ciprián's reflexes and level of attention were less than the woman's? Does it make sense that any degree of alcohol in the blood automatically makes the motor abilities of any individual inferior to those of a person who hasn't consumed? Who can tell me she wasn't distracted with something else? Who can tell me whether or not she was even comfortable driving a car?

There was one death, I agree, and those who seemed to be at fault came out ahead. How would the situation have been interpreted if the positions of the cars were inverted? What would people have said if Ciprián, his son, and Rita had died instead of her?

I don't have that information and I probably never will. All I did was to get his priorities straight. Whatever happened, it's a thing of the past. It didn't make sense for Ciprián to turn himself in and at the same time bring both of his families to ruin. It didn't make sense to imprison me either, when I have no absolute control over his actions. What good could it make to put me in jail?

Those who were really affected were the relatives of the dead woman. They lost a loved one and would suffer the consequences in the long term. It was better to forget them and not raise suspicions. Besides, I didn't want to deal with the risk that Ciprián's heart would soften enough to do something stupid like admitting his guilt. No, you can't look back on life.

The topic was never mentioned again. He had to move on with his life.

As the years passed, his lodge kept growing. What had started out as a handful of old farts with no clue of what to do with their lives, had transformed into a vibrant body rich in young blood with an entrepreneurial spirit. The prestige the lodge was said to have long ago had been restored and one could argue, surpassed.

For the most part, the lodge became a success because of Ciprián's energy and vitality. He gave it new life. He was a symbol of inspiration to its members: coming from poverty and turning into a businessman, performing acts of heroism, putting up a political front in favor of a growing opposition. His example motivated others to find out how to do more, to work for their society.

Many brother freemasons wanted to recognize Ciprián for everything he had done to raise the lodge from the ground, which is why they supported him to lead it. Ciprián certainly was in favor of the idea and was willing to occupy the chair. He felt there was still more potential for growth and to visibly impact the city's quality of life. If he wasn't able to do it from the mayor's office, he would do it from the lodge.

Naturally, not everyone thought this was a good idea. Having such a strong candidate running on the masonic ballot would crush the aspirations of some high-level veterans. I had the impression that, behind closed doors, Ciprián was being conspired against to be taken out of the race.

The old man who recruited him, whom Ciprián—armed with a can of tomato sauce—had saved from a sure beating more than twenty years back, came to talk to him. He looked as wrinkly and pale as ever.

"Ciprián, you have helped us get to where we are now. You've done a great job," the old man said. Ciprián had to stick his ears to the man's mouth in order to hear him.

"Gosh, I thank you for those words. If it hadn't been for you, I probably would have never had the chance to join—" Ciprián said, but the old man interrupted him.

"Many brother freemasons have commented that you have been seeing a woman out of wedlock. Is this true?" the old man said.

"Well—" Ciprián began to reply, but was again interrupted. Evidently, the man was deaf.

"You need to choose one!" the old man said, raising his voice. He had been sent as a messenger by some coward who didn't want to face him. Not surprisingly, the big boss and his side-kicks were observing the conversation from the back of the room. Ciprián left the old man and headed toward them.

"You can't make me do that," Ciprián said to the group. Their position compromised and their plot uncovered, they began to scatter around like pigeons.

"Ciprián, how could we discuss with others about ethics, about the voyage that is learning to control the vices and passions that oppress our intellectual selves? It is impossible for us to keep you if you are not representing what the lodge stands for. You need to decide which one you will keep!" the old man continued, as he reached Ciprián.

"If what you want is for me to leave so that you can take over everything, then I'll leave!" Ciprián said loudly, in front of everybody. From that moment on, he had renounced membership to the lodge.

Celín, now his ex-brother freemason, sat with him one afternoon to discuss his resignation as gentlemen would: Ciprián drowning in worries and rum.

"I'm not ready to make that decision and they have no right to get into my business," Ciprián said. He wasn't ready and he didn't want to be ready. How could he resign to one of them? It would have caused more harm than good. They were not even close to being the happiest women in the universe, but they weren't doing that bad considering the hole they had been digging themselves into over the years.

"They're jealous because you have two women and they only have one," Celín said.

"What will happen to Gala if I leave her? What will happen to the kids? What about Rita?" Ciprián asked to the wind. Gala was the queen of the house, but with four children, no job, and no education, she would have a hard time supporting herself or finding a husband willing to do it for her. He also didn't want to see Rita, a single mistress with a child at risk of being a bastard if Ciprián so desired, falling victim to the same misfortune.

"Whores. No other option!" Celín said, striking his glass against the bar counter.

"I also don't want to have to see the face of some prick pretending to be the father of my children and talking shit about me!" Ciprián said. Malicious gossipers would categorize Ciprián as an asshole, but in all truth he supported two families that would have otherwise not fared as well on their own. In return, it was a way for him to keep satisfied both his physical and family needs, because the remaining option would have been to leave everything behind and start with a new woman from scratch. But to what end? To have yet another one to support?

"Wait, where's your kid?" Celín asked. He turned around looking for him among the pool tables. "Quique! Come and read me the poem."

Once the owner of a popular restaurant next to Ciprián's gasoline station, Celín now spent his afternoons reciting love poems for a radio show. That was one of the ways in which he paid for his drinking.

Quique helped him memorize the poems. He read them out loud to Celín two or three times just before he went to the radio station, which was only a few steps away from the bar. Rum gave him super memory powers because, with only two or three repetitions, he was ready to show up at the station. Ciprián and Quique stayed at the bar and listened to the transmission. He recited the poem with such a deep and passionate voice that he sounded like a soap opera hunk.

Ever since he sold the restaurant, Celín had been going through some rough financial problems. He sold it simply because he wanted to work less, so he found himself a job as a school bus driver. Although at the time he owned the restaurant he made deposits to his Social Security account, the profits he made the last few years before selling it were invested on drinking and gambling, two bad habits he never managed to overcome.

When he came back from the radio station, he seemed worried. Apparently, somebody had reminded him of a problem he had.

"Chepo, I need help," Celín said.

"What happened? Why the long face?" Ciprián asked.

"I hadn't mentioned it before, but I'm getting close to retirement and I'm still five hundred dollars short of getting full benefits. It's five hundred I don't have," Celín replied.

"I can give you money. You're like my brother!" Ciprián said. Before Ciprián even offered the money, he was sure Celín wouldn't make the deposit and would drink it all within a few weeks. Nevertheless, he wanted to give him a hand.

"Thank you, brother. May God repay you in blessings!" Celín said.

"It's no big deal. If it hadn't been for hungry truckers, I probably wouldn't have gotten any clients!" Ciprián said.

CHAPTER XIV

Man of few words

Ciprián went by Rita's house two or three times per week, normally Tuesdays, Thursdays, and Fridays. They had been seeing each other for so many years that their affair had turned into a way of life. Rita seemed content. She never asked for Ciprián to abandon neither Gala nor his children. She never showed any hatred or spite against them. She never asked him for more time together or for any luxuries. Ciprián never promised her anything, either. However, they both seemed to arrive to the understanding that he would always support her as long as she was content with being marginalized by society's norms and would commit herself to respect them to the letter.

Was it that she thought she had a better life that way? Perhaps. She had her space and more time away from Ciprián, which gave her the chance to reflect about her disagreements with him or about life and the spirit. Who knows what else she did with her free time? The important thing was that she had more time for herself. Perhaps it wasn't such a bad deal if compared to spending every waking hour with the same person, revisiting pointless fights and arguments, slowly annihilating and gutting out whatever love and passion flowered the first day they met.

Did she maybe enjoy having time to dress up, make herself beautiful, go for a night out and be admired by Ciprián?—as opposed to Gala, who wore a robe most of the time and reeked of garlic? Perhaps she loved hearing him complain about his marriage or his business concerns without having to worry about solving any of them? Perhaps she enjoyed how Ciprián so passionately rid himself of his sexual frustrations while he was with her? Perhaps she enjoyed being at full liberty to cheat on Ciprián if she so desired?

They lived in a small wooden house, which was considerably humbler than the first house Ciprián bought when he married Gala. She had small buckets strategically scattered around the house collecting water drops that filtered from the ceiling. Highways of termites ran up the walls, persistently reconstructing their roads on a weekly basis after seeing them being stripped out by Rita's violent spatula. Drywood termites took care of feasting on the rest of the house inside out. Every time Rita moved furniture to mop the floor, she heard the subtle whisper of wood turned into sand running from one end to the other.

When Ciprián arrived, he sat on his armchair to eat mandarin oranges. Quique welcomed him enthusiastically; he was eager to take advantage of what little time he got to spend with his part-time father. He bathed him in hugs and kisses. He told him about his day, his school, his teacher.

Quique normally brought the newspaper and read him the news, just as Ciprián did for his father so many times before. He would lay the newspaper on the floor and would get on all fours, like a small dog, to read. Ciprián took his shoes off and rested his feet over his back like a king with his peon. While he listened to Quique read, he unpeeled the mandarin oranges with his hands and handed him some every other article he read.

Though Ciprián had already scattered his sodium bicarbonate and sugar formula traps around the house, he wouldn't stop staring at the ceiling. He still hadn't recovered from that infamous day in which, from that same ceiling weakened by humidity and drywood termites, pieces of rotten wood began falling over his head and lap, followed by dozens of the biggest and fattest Coca Cola-colored cockroaches he had ever seen. Hairy, pointy little feet ran around his body, through his hair, and under his clothes. He tried to sweep them off with his hands but they held onto his fingers, climbed up his arms hurriedly until reaching his elbows, and sneaked in from under his sleeves.

"Help me! Get them off me!" Ciprián cried out. He was terrified of cockroaches, especially those that flew erratically around the room.

"I'm trying to, but there are just too many of them!" Quique said, while he rolled a newspaper and began beating his father with it.

"Gimme just one moment, and we'll get rid of them in a heartbeat. Here. You sweep his back, and I'll sweep his front," Rita said, showing up in the living room armed with two brooms. Mother and child swept Ciprián from head to toe while he kept beating himself each time he felt tickles inside his pants.

Until that moment, they weren't aware they had been sharing their attic with a giant colony of flying cockroaches, which used it to hide comfortably in the darkness during the day and ran around restlessly at night, waving their disgusting antennae across every nook and cranny of the house, over ears, between eyes, across the mouth, and into the nose.

Around that time, Ciprián began his next entrepreneurial experiment upon entering into the port and opening a container coming from New York. He normally got Impala and Trans Am cars, which was what he sold at his dealership those days, but this time he found the Cherokee, an incredibly cool single-engine airplane painted with red and white stripes. He had ordered it so that his new business associate, with whom he would meet up that day to try it out, could use it.

"I'm going to make one trip per day to the Dominican Republic and I'll come back with three Dominicans per trip. You'll get your commission at the end of each week," the associate said, while he combed his hair. This man would pioneer the style of pointy neck shirts and brown-shaded sunglasses popular back in the seventies.

"How is it that you get paid?" Ciprián said, while the man circled the plane. He was looking looked for imperfections or screws that could go loose during flight.

"I get paid here. I know some people who want to bring their friends or families here and they give me the money. Once that part is done, we start talking about flying," the associate said.

"Do you have any partners in the Dominican Republic?" Ciprián asked.

"Of course I do. I have two or three of them. They pick passengers up and bring them to the runway. That way I can fly out of there quickly," the associate said.

"Won't it be difficult for you to come back into the island? Can't they detect you by radar or something like that?" Ciprián asked. They had gotten inside the plane. It was his first time inside one. He watched all the buttons and handles the pilot touched as they prepared for takeoff.

"That won't be a problem. It's a small plane. All I need to do is to fly low when I start getting close to the island. The radar will be blind," his associate said.

"So, what happens after you land? You just let them loose and they start running?" Ciprián said.

"No! I'd get caught pretty quickly if I did that. We always land on a runway in San Sebastián. There's nobody around there, but if the police catches one of those Dominicans and he talks, we won't last long," the associate said.

"Then, how do you do it? Do you have people helping you here?" Ciprián asked.

"After I land, a car comes to take them somewhere far away where they can meet up with their family," the associate said.

"Well, seems like you know what you're doing," Ciprián said. What if something went wrong? He didn't need to know. The more he knew, the more he got involved. Besides, at that precise moment he was more worried about how fast they were moving away from firm soil. "Take good care of her for me, now."

"Hold on a minute. You do know how to pilot this thing, don't you?" the associate asked.

"Not at all. That's your job," Ciprián said.

"You need to learn, Chepo. Imagine what people will think when they find out that you have an airplane you don't fly. It would be suspicious, wouldn't it?" the associate said.

"Ah, shit! I have to learn?" Ciprián said. What if the engine stopped working? What if another airplane crashed into him? What if his landing approach was too fast? What if his instructor died of a heart attack all of a sudden? Fear crept into Ciprián.

"Take some lessons. I'm only going to be using the plane during the evenings and I'll leave it available for you at the airport. Just make sure you finish using it before five. Is that OK?" the associate asked.

"Alright. I'll try not to crash it!" Ciprián said. The mind-block gave him goosebumps and battered his stomach. It was an uncomfortable feeling, but I had to make him feel it in response to what his body kept screaming at me: bad idea!

In spite of his nerves overtaking him during his first airplane voyage, Ciprián was determined to learn how to fly. His second time was completely different. The definition his body had with respect to the concept of fear had evolved. The initial feeling of vertigo lessened and would keep doing so until completely vanishing, letting him finally enjoy the greatness of his surroundings.

On one side, he admired the limitless dark blues of the ocean merging with the turquoise waters of the shallow coast, before being smashed into pieces by the imposing barrier reefs, and gently bathed the pristine and refined sands of their beaches.

On another side, he had the greenery of the countryside, randomly undulated by creeks, rivers, and hills. The mountains rising in the distance looked to deceive, forming an alliance with the cloudscape surrounding them to selfishly deny him the view of the not so distant southern coast.

"What's that down there?" Ciprián asked the instructor. He pointed toward a white dish hiding nested in a basin. It was surrounded by hills in the shape of egg cartons, covered in rainforest.

"That's the Arecibo radio-telescope, the one they finished building a couple of years back. It has a diameter of about three hundred meters. They say it's the biggest one in the world," the instructor said.

"That piece of crap is three hundred meters wide? It's no bigger than a quarter, from this high up!" Ciprián said.

"Gives you an idea just how high we're flying," the instructor said.

"It looks more like a dish than a telescope," Ciprián said.

"It does. You don't look through a lens. You're supposed to see using radio waves. The waves hit objects in space and get reflected back to the dish. That way, they can figure out the shape of planets or get other types of signals from outer space," the instructor said. One of his hands was wide open, simulating the dish, while the other one was closed in a fist, simulating a planet. He moved his hands, one toward the other, sort of complementing what he said. "The most useful thing about it is that it can be used it to spy on the Russians."

"Good! We have to keep a good eye on the Russians," Ciprián said.

Rita wasn't at all glad to find out through gossip that his lover now owned an airplane. She waited for him, sitting on the sofa, trying to conceal the rage within.

"You mean to tell me that while my house falls apart, you're flying around on your own airplane?" Rita asked, irate.

"Just which plane are you referring to?" Ciprián asked. Stupid reaction. Who would think of coming up with something like that?

"Do I look like an idiot to you?" Rita asked. He had never seen her so angry. Now, how would he justify purchasing an airplane?

Anyone who didn't know the truth would consider that investment as the indulgence of a wealthy man. Even Ciprián would have thought so and surely Rita did. It wasn't until he flew it for the first time that he removed that stigma from his head. Now he saw it as yet another way to challenge himself, to take control over his mind and body.

To me it was more than that. Flying an airplane was something many wouldn't even consider doing. It was gaining a completely new perspective on the world and its surroundings. Touching ground now felt mundane, common. He would never respond the same way to the stimuli in life because he had felt something so much more overwhelming.

"I wanted to surprise you, dear, but the surprise is now ruined," Ciprián said. He had to come up with something. He couldn't give her a philosophical explanation for his actions, and much less tell her the truth. He couldn't turn her into an accomplice.

"What do you mean 'surprise'?" Rita said, putting her eyebrows together. She took the bait.

"Yes, a surprise. I rented that plane. I was taking some lessons so I could take you up into the sky with me, my love," Ciprián said.

That story lasted a few months, during which time got his pilot's license and spent his time going on recreational flights with his two women and their respective children. His associate continued with the nightly commercial use of the aircraft, but he found himself in a bind one night after the police arrested the driver of his transport vehicle. There were three passengers with him.

Ciprián, an emergency resort, found himself that night parked in front of the famed clandestine runway in San Sebastián. He was sitting on top of the hood of his car, waiting to transport three illegal aliens to an empty parking lot in Aguadilla, praying to God that the police wouldn't find him. It was 3:45 in the morning and the plane hadn't shown up.

"Is it common for him to be so late?" Ciprián asked.

"No," the man next to him replied.

His associate had described him as 'the man in charge of security'. He would ride with him on the car. He had a gun, 'just in case'.

"He was supposed to be here an hour ago. What are we supposed to do now?" Ciprián asked.

"We wait," he said. He was a man of few words.

The man pointed his finger at a small light in the distance. Ciprián recognized the growl of his Cherokee's engine as it approached the runway. But something was wrong. The plane wasn't slowing down and its nose wasn't going up. It kept getting closer and closer until it was too late to straighten it. The nose was the first thing that hit the ground; the propeller blades shoveled up the grass runway, shooting slices of earth into the air, some of which even struck Ciprián's car two hundred meters away.

An explosion.

Before it got to a full stop, the plane was already covered in flames, revealing among the darkness the silhouettes of bodies desperately looking to escape. The door opened. A man jumped out and fell to the ground but quickly stood up and ran into the woods. Then a second man jumped out, in flames. He fell onto the ground and tried to stand up but couldn't. He stopped moving, consumed by fire.

Ciprián and the man of few words hurried toward the crash site. The man burning up in flames was the pilot, his associate. He was dead.

"Leave," the man of few words said. He took out his gun and disappeared into the woods.

Ciprián approached the plane, searching for survivors. The stench was nauseating, with thick fusions of flesh, hide, and sulfur emanating from the two bodies he found in the back seat of the plane. The first was that of a black man, shirtless and shoeless. He was in flames. One piece of glass pierced his neck while another was stuck between his ribs. The second body was smaller, like that of a child. It was completely charred. There was no hair left. Ciprián tried to make out his nose, mouth, eyes, and ears but he couldn't. All which made him human seemed to have molded itself into the shape of his head, making unrecognizable that poor creature. He couldn't hold his tears.

He heard shots being fired from within the woods.

"Shit," Ciprián said. He couldn't stand there waiting to see what happened or who came. Explosions? Dead people? Shots fired? All of that which he saw around him wasn't for him. He wasn't even supposed to be there. At that moment, he was supposed to by sleeping quietly, completely unaware of that madness. "Fuck this," he said, exhaling. He got in his car and rushed away from the scene of the crash.

The next day, he woke up baffled. He still couldn't believe what he had witnessed the night before. He still had the disgusting stench of sulfur stuck to his nose. Inside his car, he found an envelope with a note and cash. The note was written in terrible cursive. He didn't recognize who had written it. Who could it have been?

«This week's payment plus the cost of the Cherokee.»

Straight to the point. Only one person could have written it: the man of few words.

CHAPTER XV
Excuses to live
Margarita's diary: April 23, 1961

He still lurks from within the mirror. The dark shadow projected by the obscure man who's been keeping me company for as long as I can remember, still hasn't gone away. At the beginning I was weaker and more naive, more susceptible to his suggestions and harassments. I was scared, shaky, my mind would go blank and I just cried. It took me years to control myself and face the mirror, his abode. I celebrated my moment of triumph. The shadow stopped wanting to impose his will on me with his constant whispering at my ear, something he did every morning when he found I was alone looking at him. He kept trying to force me to kill.

My victory was short-lived. The shadow had no intention to surrender so easily. He came back at me thundering. He wanted me to know that he was more powerful than me and that even if I was under the belief that I had gained strength, he would be better prepared for combat. He would make his wrath be felt until I decided to desist. I was his slave at his mercy. He made me want to vanish from this world with all my heart, to leave behind all those wretched things that held me by the neck and suffocated me.

My own weakness has kept me alive, my own fear. The mere sight of blood running around the contour of my wrist made me stop. What a disappointment! My most valiant effort to fade away from existence turned out to be a total failure. The worst thing is that I stopped not because I saw an end to my suffering, or because I saw a bright future ahead of me, or because of my faith, or even my sense of moral and ethics. I stopped simply because I didn't feel capable of bearing the pain I would have had to suffer before I bled myself dry and finally died.

I'm lucky to be alive. After that day, I've gradually been able to coexist with him. I stopped listening to him when he says nasty things to me. My response to the pressure he puts on me has now become: "I hear you. I understand what you want and how you feel, but go away!"

However, he touched me today. I felt him touch my back. He pressed his finger firmly onto it from my left shoulder. Then, he started to go down without stopping, still pressing firmly, stinging until drawing a perfect parabola. As he finished on my right shoulder, I felt the creepy tickle of his razor-sharp nail caressing me as he relieved the pressure. It was a sign. He was telling me that I am no longer needed, that I am ready to die.

I agree. Perhaps my time has come but I can't listen to him. My life is not the same as it was before. In the past, I was alone, lost in my thoughts, relying on everyone with no one relying on me. Things are different now. I've met a man who loves me and is willing to accept me as I am, imperfect. We will get married. We will make a family together. I can't die now; I'm not ready. I'm engaged now. Ángel is so good to me, so patient with me. I love him dearly and he loves me back. Any harm I make to myself will harm him as well and I'm not willing to do that.

He wants to have children. He wants a lot of children. Five, to be precise. Three boys and two girls, if possible. I don't know what to do. I would love to please him but children make everything more difficult. I also have my own dreams and desires. I would start with two. That way, I'll have more time to practice playing the piano. Otherwise, if I don't get time to practice, I'll never become famous. My tours around the island and, God willing, internationally, will keep me busy.

I'm quite worried about that because I'm not sure how to find some middle ground between my dream and Ángel's. He wants to have so many kids and I don't want to get in the way of that. He's a man, so I must respect his wishes. For the moment I won't say anything. That was my mother's advice, not to say anything so that he doesn't get mad at me; let him have the first and second child first and then see if he changes his mind over time. He should hold off on the third one on his own accord.

No, I need to keep ignoring the man behind the mirror at any cost.

Dad says what's happening to me—that I'm having such feelings— is a good thing. He says it makes me a better and more resilient person. I agree with him in that I'm becoming a better person but I think I can do more than just to bear the burden. I want to help others going through the same ordeal. I've been through the same pains and fears. I can give them advice to get over them.

Besides, my advice wouldn't be limited to those who are suffering like me, but would extend to those taking care of them. Family can make a huge difference. My mother is a pretty good example. She has changed so much and I feel I can count on her so much more. She understands how I'm feeling and is now more aware of what she tells me and how. She stopped asking me to be strong; she knows I've been fighting hard and that I'm tired. Now she prepares some hot baths for me that make me feel better and tells me to take a break, to slow down and take my time.

I still feel some resentment toward her. I can't forgive her maternal ineptitude. It's not easy to erase decades of abandonment and psychological abuse. From the get-go, she should have known how to take care of me and, if she didn't, she should have figured it out. There's no valid excuse not to do it. However, it might be a bit too much to ask her to pay for mistakes she committed in the past even if I know the person behind them is still there and could resurge at any moment. I think it's better to pretend everything is alright and that we're getting along well. I love her and I know that changing her behavior toward me has been no easy task.

Dad, on the other hand, understands me better. He took me out today for a drive around the countryside. He told me I seemed too worried, that a little bit of sunlight and fresh air would do me well, that the house wasn't the best place for me to be.

I believe him. It's just that at home I often feel like I can't breathe, and I struggle catch some air to prevent suffocation. I find myself alone in my room surrounded by walls and objects foreign to me. I feel lost, in the wrong house, unable to quiet down the screeching, high-pitched silence that whistles in my ear.

Being outside, breathing fresh air, and getting sprinkled by sunshine makes me so happy! Everything smells sweet, like mango juice.

We sat on a big rock overlooking the mountains. He spoke about my uncle, whom I never got the chance to meet. He said that, at twenty-eight years old, my uncle still behaved like a child. He spent his time sitting on a chair, dulled, laughing at anything, or singing church songs. Apparently, he had a beautiful voice because many people came to church just to hear him sing.

That was news to me. I was aware I had an uncle who died before I was born but that was pretty much it. Dad and my grandparents didn't talk about those things because they were very painful memories. The family went through very hard times. When I was a little girl my uncle was always present, but only as the mysterious family member whom everyone wanted to erase from memory. Evidence of his existence lay hidden within family albums buried in the attic, under old belongings and newspapers turned yellow by time. There were dozens of black and white pictures of my parents, baptisms of older cousins, and family gatherings. Handicapped as he was, that dead fellow shared many moments of happiness between his family and friends completely unaware that he would succumb to death shortly after.

Nobody knew for certain his cause of death. Grandma told dad she had been able to speak to her son through a woman who could connect with spirits, a medium. My grandmother sat at a round table full of people having the same vehement need she had to communicate with dead relatives. The medium had a face like a prune, wrinkled by time. She would start by shouting out ideas and describing random visions of spirits until someone related personally to what was being said. My grandmother got chosen that day. The woman yelled and struck my grandmother's forehead. She fell on her back, supported by two women waiting to lay her on the floor, as the medium and the rest of the people around the table prayed.

Grandma doesn't remember that part when she was lying on the floor. She felt as if she had been asleep. She only remembers that, upon waking up, the medium revealed to her how her son had died. It had been the medicine. The medicine the doctor prescribed for an illness that wasn't supposed to be grave was too strong. His body couldn't take it. The doctor made a mistake and his bad judgment killed her first-born son.

Dad suffered a lot from his brother's death. He felt he needed to distract himself, to put his grieving aside and carry on with his life. There was little else to do if there was no way to bring his brother back. As is customary for many, his work became his sanctuary. He put long hours into finalizing mundane tasks and abandoned projects he couldn't have cared less for in the past.

At the time, nobody at the office knew about his brother's death. His boss was ecstatic given he was doing such a great job. He wouldn't stop complimenting my dad in front of his colleagues, treating him to lunch, and assigning him new and challenging projects. Dad said he was so proud of getting so many compliments for his work; it was a huge confidence boost. That's when everything he did and the way he did it became the optimal way, the perfect way. His colleagues, with their weak ideas and half-finished projects, were no match for him. They were always distracted by personal issues and didn't put as much thought into things as he did. He secretly mocked them. He was certain that given the opportunity to complete any of his colleague's tasks, he could complete them successfully and with minimal effort.

Over time, he started noticing how his colleagues began distancing themselves from his desk. They stopped coming to chat with him, or to joke around, or to get him to go out for lunch with them. He convinced himself they envied his skills, which is why they didn't want to be around him. However, he wouldn't let that get to him. If they didn't want to be with him, he didn't want to be with them. He decided to go out for lunch an hour later to avoid any odd moments as the clock got closer to noon. After a few days, he noticed that the change saved him at least thirty minutes of waiting lines and delayed service because of all the people who came out for lunch at the same time. In addition to that, an empty office gave him a full hour completely free of distractions to concentrate. Upon reaching this conclusion, he smiled. His so-called colleagues, selfishly attempting to exclude him from their social circle, had no idea what they were missing out on work efficiency.

Soon enough, the quality of his work began to decline. His pride and ego didn't allow him to get help when he needed it. He blamed himself if something went wrong, even if it had been something he had no control over. He punished himself by putting more hours and effort into his work until things were fixed, while he kept his composure in front of his co-workers at all times. Nevertheless, the more blame he put on himself, the more aware of his mistakes he became, and the more things went wrong.

It wasn't until he lost control of his mind that he realized the gravity of his situation. Simple arithmetic became an impossible task. Answering the phone, an easy everyday task, made him panic. He left the phone ringing and ringing. Who wanted to speak to him? Why? What if he couldn't get the information the person needed? What if he gave them the wrong information? That was his job, though. He had to answer. He pushed himself to take the phone confidently and listen, regardless of the consequences. He would say nothing. Panic. Trembling. Blushing. Muteness.

He had to be transferred to another department. Things started out well there, he said. He stopped feeling the panic he felt before his colleagues and clients. However, he became too friendly, too sociable. He talked to everyone, even to people who had nothing to do with the work he was doing but went there to do other errands. He tried to speak to them, to be friendly and funny. He always got back courtesy smiles and small chat, followed by an uncomfortable step back as dad tried to continue conversing. He thought they probably weren't used to so much attention from a stranger.

He told me I was born around the time when he had been transferred to that position. He held my hands and I could see the sadness in his eyes, as if everything he had just told me had been a prelude to a terrible truth. He told me he always meant to apologize for never wanting to spend time with me or mom, for his weakness, and for not being the best father. Playing with me and seeing me grow up were all things that he missed. I was a permanent nuisance, an additional burden to his day.

His vulnerability also prevented him from showing any affection to mom; he didn't speak to her. During those years, he never shared his feelings with her; he didn't even argue with her. He only took on, as he sat on his armchair dispirited, the cries and complaints of a woman with whom he shared the same roof but whom he had left living by herself. He insisted that it had been my mom who took care of me during my childhood and that he took no part in any of it.

Before we headed back home, he told me that despite his wrongdoings as a father and husband, he never stopped loving us. His love never withered, kept him going, dispelled the demon that wanted to take him away, and kept him alive.

CHAPTER XVI
The file

A police officer walked into Ciprián's office days after his plane was reduced to ashes. Ciprián knew him well, since he opened up the gas station and signed the agreement with the police car fleet. It was the same police officer who filled out the report on that embarrassing car accident in front of his wife's house while traveling with Rita and Quique. He came in and greeted the employees, joking around a bit, as usual. He must have done it to keep the appearance of normalcy because his face changed as soon as they were behind closed doors.

"Ciprián, we have a problem," the police officer said.

More problems! Why is he here? Had he linked him to the plane, to the man of few words? He got the heebie jeebies. He had to calm down. No one would be able to recognize the wrecked plane.

"In life we never have problems, only situations. Tell me. What's the matter?" Ciprián asked. Lies. They were problems. There's a reason why the word existed.

"You're being investigated," the police officer said. He placed a dark brown file with a label in a corner on his desk that said: Ciprián Santiesteban. Ciprián opened the file and the first things he saw inside were old pictures of his electoral campaign for the mayor's office.

"1960? Since the elections?" Ciprián asked.

There was a list of all the business agreements he had signed over a decade; it detailed the full name of each government official who signed them. There were pictures of him shaking hands with them. All of his business partners were listed. Among them Felix stood out, who had been a key supporter during the elections and who suddenly had to move to a new life in New York, becoming Ciprián's automobile importer.

He glanced through reports signed by old brother freemasons —trusted men whom he considered friends—in which they gave an account of their interactions with Ciprián: what he said, what he did, who he was with, and the times and dates of each encounter. Ciprián had gone out for drinks and family gatherings with these people, celebrated birthdays and holidays with them. They were spies!

With regards to the Cherokee, his main concern at the time, they only knew that he had purchased it and occasionally flew it. Fortunately, they knew nothing more.

"Yeah. It seems to me that when you ran for mayor, you gave them quite a scare and they probably didn't want to be taken by surprise again," the police officer said.

"But this was more than ten years ago! I'm not even thinking of running again!" Ciprián shouted, closing the file and throwing it on top of the desk.

"I don't know. They must still keep it in case you change your mind. People know you and things are going well for you. Besides, their party has been getting weaker and weaker over the years; they're not going to win another quarter. They must be desperate," the police officer said.

"Do you know what they're planning to do with that? Are they going to keep stalking me until I decide to run again and then start harassing and threatening me?" Ciprián asked.

"I don't know what their plans are but none of my guys knew about this. If we came to know now, it's because there's something cooking," the police officer said.

"Like what? Are they planning to take me out before I even decide to run? What am I supposed do about that?" Ciprián asked.

"Well, the thing is, you're not the only one involved in this, Chepo. If you fall, many around you will fall as well," the police officer said. He leaned over the desk toward Ciprián and lowered his voice. "The guys at the station, especially those who don't know you as well as I do, are not going to keep supporting you. I can't do it either. We're going to be in deep shit if anything points our direction during the investigation. Do you understand? I have a wife and kids, just like you, and I can't take any part of these things."

"Then, how can we prevent this investigation from happening? What do we do?" Ciprián asked, after a long pause.

"See, this term 'we' implies many people need to do something. Now, what can 'you' do? That's the right question. If I were you, I'd do whatever it takes to get out of here before it's too late. Find a place where you won't be a menace to them and leave. I'm sure they'll leave you alone," the police officer said.

That file had gotten the best of him. He had few friends left. He didn't know whom he could trust anymore. It was also clear that the municipal police would cease to cover up his secrets or look out for his interests. Had he gotten stubborn and decided to stay, he would have been followed, spied on, and threatened not only by those who had been behind his every step for the past decade, but also by those who covered up his secrets in the past and would somehow be incriminated if a proper investigation were to take place.

Besides, only a few days had gone by since the incident with the Cherokee. Although it was an unlikely possibility, what would have happened if he was linked to the plane crash? Putting aside any legal consequences, was his life in danger because of what he knew? Could the man of few words be the last thing he would see in his life?

He wasn't about to make his life more complicated than it already was.

"So, you're moving to Río Piedras?" Simón asked. He still could not believe the news his cousin had given him. Río Piedras was to give him asylum from the dangers that came to threaten him in his hometown.

"We're going to be OK there. Although I hadn't had to make the decision until today, I had been thinking about moving there for a long time. What I wasn't expecting was to have to do it so soon," Ciprián said.

"You should be safer there. It's a big city with many people. Nobody knows you there or cares about what you do," Simón said, but then he paused before continuing to speak. "What are you planning to do with your businesses?"

"There's little left to do. I accepted an offer for the gas station land lot. I should also be able to sell off any cars left at the dealer by the end of the month. I can give a car to Pablo or Irma if I don't manage to sell them," Ciprián said.

"What about the warehouse?" Simón asked. His concern was evident in his face. It had been something that they had built together after all, but that Ciprián owned.

"We need to talk about that in the next couple of days. I was thinking to transfer it over to you at cost. After all, you've been taking care of it on your own for quite a while now; it's as much yours as it is mine!" Ciprián said.

"You know I wouldn't be opposed to that. Will you start something up over there?" Simón asked.

"Of course! I still have plenty of years left in me before I need to retire! I'm planning to start up a gardening store," Ciprián said.

"You always have something under your sleeve, huh?" Simón said.

"I've spoken to a few farm owners and got them to sell me plants, seeds, and pots in different sizes so I can re-sell them in San Juan," Ciprián said.

"That sounds good. With all the new houses they've been building everywhere there..." Simón said.

"Exactly. I also teamed up with a Mexican living here to import a lot of terrace and patio artwork from Mexico: from ceramic vases and other handcrafts to fountains and life-sized statues. He says you can get many things for cheap over there. It's a good way to differentiate ourselves from the rest," Ciprián said.

"A Mexican? Ha, ha. You're crazy!" Simón said.

"Ha, ha," Ciprián said, taking the keys to his car out of his pockets and smacking them against his thighs. "Alright, I'm off. Take good care of mom, OK?"

"Beware of evil women there. Don't let them trap you!" Simón said, as he hugged him and patted his back.

"Don't joke around like that. You know I'm a serious man," Ciprián said, winking an eye at him, his smile revealing a pair of teeth made out of gold.

"Hey, and what are you planning to do with Rita and her kid? Are you also taking them with you?" Simón asked.

"Not yet. I already spoke to her. She wasn't happy to hear the news, but it is what it is. I told her that as soon as things start going well for me there, I'll bring her and the kid," Ciprián said.

The truth was that, when his mistress got the news, she was pale, lacking the strength and confidence that she had always maintained. Perhaps she thought she had lost everything she had accomplished with him, as if the world had crashed on top of her. Her man would move out to a new city with his family, to a new house and a new life, changing her whole world and leaving her alone. Was he doing it to forget his past and begin from scratch? Could he be able to forget the times they had together and leave her and his son behind? Spending now more time alone with Gala, was reconciliation possible? Was it possible to try to heal the wounds of his cancerous and passionless marriage?

She had absolutely nothing to worry about. Had Ciprián wanted to leave her, he would have done so already.

He bought a big corner house in Río Piedras. It was in one of those new high-end neighborhoods sprouting up fast in the metropolitan area. The back porch and the ample gardens of the house became a sanctuary for Gala. She took advantage of Ciprián's new gardening venture to fall in love with all kinds of plants and flowers, especially orchids. She spent hours sweeping leaves, gathering the ripe fruit that fell from the imposing *jobo* tree on the backyard, fertilizing soil, watering and trimming plants, weeding, and transferring plants from small pots to big ones. She soon gave life, color, and character to every corner of the new house.

The Mexican statues also had a place around the property. In the garden in front of the house she put two: the first one being a stone creature with the body of a man and open wings that, after no one knowing what to make of it, was named Mayan god; the second one was that of an armless muse, aptly named Venus.

The Mayan god was the guardian of the home, centered in front of the stairwell leading to the second floor, where the house's main entrance was located. The muse was set in a corner, distracted in her eyes among the small pink flowers of the high and lush bush next to her.

In the backyard garden, a third statue was set: another Venus. She didn't end up between the orchids or under the lordly protection of the *jobo* tree, but on the greens located to the side of the house. I was a narrow area, on a slope severely punished by the sun. If not even lizards wanted to wander around there, much less would have pondering souls. The Venus was set there, bored, and admired never more.

Gala's afternoons were spent resting on her balcony, which extended along the front of the house supported by three columns that made up the garage on the first floor. She watched as cars went past and neighbors went in and out of their houses; she watched airplanes getting lost among mountains in the distance; she witnessed as greens, road tar, and concrete battled to the death for land's domain.

She wasn't always in complete solitude. There was always someone around, be it Willie or Pey, who lived there until they graduated from college, or Irma and Pablo, who sat there with her whenever they came by to visit. Even after Willie and Pey moved out, she gave board to a renter or a distant relative looking to study at the university. What never failed was that anyone who came in or out had to spend at least a few minutes conversing with her on the balcony.

At that time, Río Piedras was going through its golden age. It was the center of economic activity for the working class and the commercial bridge between Old San Juan and the rest of the country. At the market square, the largest one in the island, one could get anything from the vegetables that made up a good *sancocho* dish, to shoes, clothing, and electrical appliances. The country was undergoing tremendous growth and you could see it from all the commercial activity on the streets. More and more people came to buy and more and more stores opened up for business.

Ciprián began his new life opening up a gardening store but it was just that, a beginning. He knew very well that the income from a gardening store would never match those of a supermarket, a gas station and tire shop, a car dealership, and an importer of illegal immigrants from the Dominican Republic. He also knew he couldn't get into those businesses again because there was just too much competition in San Juan and its surroundings, the same big guy competition he always feared would take over Arecibo. There were already plenty of supermarket chains, gas stations, and car dealerships that were bigger than those he had. He needed to find something more exclusive, less commercialized. That's why, on a busy corner street at the very center of Río Piedras, he opened up a jewelry store.

As it was to be expected, Ciprián saw his idea as an excellent investment: purchase high volumes of non-perishable goods that increased in value over time, and from which he could gain a margin up to ten times higher than any of his previous businesses.

All he needed to take out the small jewelers in the area was a decent amount of capital and a good partner to help him get cheaper goods than any of them; he had to start out strong and gain solid footing. The capital was already in his pocket just waiting for it to be spent. His partner would be none other than his old automobile importer and good friend, Félix, who was ideally located in New York, the capital of the world. He was the only person to whom Ciprián could ever trust such a large investment.

Having gotten himself a good house for his family and having started up two solid businesses, he had only one more thing left to do: get Rita.

CHAPTER XVII

Mute keys

Margarita's diary: March 2, 1978

I 've got a piano student, after so many years! A woman came with father José María to bring him to his first class. It's a blessing. Father José María said that since I didn't want to leave my house and socialize with people, then he would bring the people to me. If Mohammed will not go to the mountain, the mountain must go to Mohammed. I have no intention of going for an unpleasant day out. I keep telling him that the doors to my home are open to anyone who wishes to visit me at any time.

I extend this invitation to my ungrateful brother, who almost never visits. He's always telling me how he doesn't have time, how hard he's working. He thinks I was born yesterday. The reason is simple: he just doesn't want to come see me. I see the mailman more than I see him. At least with this new student I've got someone to expect, someone who really wants to come see me and spend time with me.

If I was going to start giving lessons again, the first thing I had to do was to get my piano tuned. After so many years, my old tuner was so surprised to hear my voice! I hadn't called for him to take a look at my piano in a long time. When I say take a look, I mean looking with his hands. He's blind. He came here like in the good old days, wearing black sunglasses and a white *guayabera* shirt, as if he had been frozen by time since the last time I had seen him. He held his helper's hand, whose job was to take him from house to house and sit him in front of the piano with every tool necessary for the tuning job.

Long ago, my brother told me that when I wasn't there, he joked around and talked about filthy things. He asked my brother what things he had done with his girlfriends, licking his lips with a perverted giggle as my brother replied. My brother proclaimed himself an expert impersonator, making nasty expressions with his face and panting like a dog.

I doubt he's that kind of person. If he was, he never showed it around me. It's either because I have a hard time hearing or because I'm a woman, but he stayed decent around me. He was a polite and quiet person. He put all of his attention into adjusting the strings, playing them diligently one by one from left to right. He kept at it until his ears were satisfied, until the sound was perfect.

Both my brother and I agreed that despite being blind all of his life, he could play a *danza* such as 'Mis Amores' like a professional. It's because he got a lot of practice. He played the same piece every single time he was done tuning a piano. I never thought of asking him if he knew how to play something else.

When it was time to pay, his helper's job was limited to confirming the amount paid. The blind tuner took out a piece of paper from the chest pocket of his *guayabera* and read it by feeling some small holes on it with his hands, then added more holes using a special stylus made for the blind. I imagine that's how he made notes and can keep track of how much money he has in his pocket. Having a system probably helped him stay organized.

Before leaving, he gave me two naphthalene balls to protect the piano from pests and wished me luck with my student. I waved him goodbye from my balcony as he left, but then I remembered he was blind.

My student is a very intelligent child. He's had only a few lessons but I can tell he wants to learn. During the week, he practices all the homework I write on his notebook, unlike my niece who wanted to do her homework during the lesson. She thought I was stupid or something. That's why she stopped playing, just like her father did when he was a child. That's not the right way to learn.

I know that getting into it is hard. It's not easy to develop good habits in the fingers and it's very hard to see how what is being learned will evolve into complex pieces such as those from Beethoven and Chopin; don't even get me started on those impossible ones by Rachmaninoff. Technique is very important. Any student will eventually learn how to play, but if he lacks the technique—the correct placement fingers need to run up and down the keyboard and play the most challenging chords effortlessly—he will struggle to play those difficult pieces.

It's my duty as a teacher to correct his technique right from the start so that the student can develop good habits. Even I, having spent so many years working on my technique, fail simply because I lack practice. However, I can't lie to myself. I know that things will get more complicated for me as the months pass. What worries me is the risk that I won't do my best just because I'm deaf.

My ears help me as much as they can. Although I'm not able to hear every note well, I still feel the drumming as each key vibrates. However, I'm aware that's not enough. My eyes have to watch over him to compensate for deficiencies in my hearing and catch him when he makes mistakes. For the moment, it's not so complicated because he's still on the Thomson beginner books. His little hands stay within the same octave and each finger is tied to a key and a number. I only have to play the back music of each beginner's piece and watch over his playing.

The Hanon scales don't pose a problem either. I remember when I used to play the whole book from memory in only one hour! It helps build dexterity and stamina for the fingers so they don't get tired easily. It's very easy to catch him making mistakes. Anybody's fingers, when they get lazy and clumsy, look terrible as they run up and down the keyboard. The flow should come effortlessly.

Clearly, it's not all about technique; it's also about theory. For him, this is the most boring part of the lesson, even if I insist it's an essential part of the language of music. It's just as hard to master as it is English, French, or Russian. A good foundation is very important because that's the only way he will learn to play whatever is placed in front of him and recognize by ear any note played. When I was a little girl, my teacher would make me sit with my back facing the piano so that I would sing out the notes he played. Being aware that I'm so bad at reading my student's lips, that's where I have to put more effort. I need to make sure he doesn't get lazy, that he gets used to keeping the beat with his hand while reading the unrhythmical music from the Danhäuser book.

'Fur Elise' was the first respectable piano piece I learned to play as a child. I saw my ten fingers strolling freely on the keyboard, each of them doing different things; there was no way I could have consciously kept track of their movements. I followed the melody but I couldn't believe what I had before my eyes. I wasn't playing music, my fingers were. They did all the work while I just sat to watch and got lost in my own life, family, frustrations, and blessings.

From that moment, my fingers served as gatekeepers to myself, something that no *riego*, *mejunje*, *sahumerio*, protection, or mental institution has managed to do. What they asked in return throughout my whole life was for me to exercise them, to keep them fit so they could effortlessly jump around from key to key and octave to octave. That way, they wouldn't forget what they're capable of playing. Only that way could they prevent the music in their memories from fading away.

I realize now that, in that calling, I've let them down monumentally. I promised them a professional career, to delight and be admired by many. I betrayed them. I honored them by acquiring a collection of forgotten pieces, having dedicated years of effort, practice, and dedication to them. I honored them by giving them hope throughout my life, wooing them again and again with the promise that I would once again master those forgotten pieces, only to give up on them at the slightest feeling of discomfort and to neglect their way back into oblivion.

153

My fingers are disillusioned, unmotivated, and worn out. They blame me for not making the best out of their youth, for not letting them be as dexterous and as fast as they could have been. Every broken promise, every instance in which I didn't take them seriously, they've made me pay for by denying me access to myself. I never realized what was going on. I'm asking them to give me one last chance. I promise things will change for the better from now on. I pray to God that they will listen to me.

CHAPTER XVIII

Ground number eleven

Ciprián bought a house for Rita in the metropolitan area and put her to work as a saleswoman behind the glass cabinets of his jewelry store. For the most part, her work consisted on giving advice to young lovers—those soon to swear to honor the sanctity of marriage—to choose their engagement rings. This turned out to be a great move for the business. The feminine touch she brought allowed her to better connect with her clients, read their eyes, and listen to them. Like a type of psycho-sensorial alchemy—if such a term exists—she managed to turn her thoughts into the perfect diamond for each couple.

Ciprián's goal was to successfully develop a type of concubinage between his wife and mistress. Both of them knew they were sharing the same man; to deny it at this point, with children in the equation, was useless. Besides, the taboo of having a mistress, with the shame this brought to his mistress and to his wife, had all but vanished as soon as they moved to such a big city. Nobody knew them; nobody cared. Why not make the best of the situation? Why not make them help one another for the prosperity of the whole family?

Always willing to cooperate, Rita helped out at the jewelry store even though she was fully aware that most of the profit would be directed toward Gala and her children, rather than her and her child. In spite of that, she gladly did it because she knew that if her man profited, she profited. The only thing he asked of Ciprián was that he be a father to Quique. She also never showed any contempt toward Gala. She even made three dresses, two for her and one for Irma, and had Ciprián offer them as gifts. They found them so beautiful and well made! They were delighted. Irma, especially, blindly saw it as a nice gesture from a loving father. Naturally, they never found out where the dresses came from.

It had to be that way because Gala never willingly took part of the concubinage. As always, she had to be deceived into cooperating rather than her simply accepting things as they were.

His wife had to be told to prepare lunch for two so that Ciprián and Rita could have a quick, tasty lunch, thus letting them work more and sell more. Gala would have exploded if she would have been told the second serving was for Rita, so Ciprián had to make Pablo his accomplice. Fortunately, she didn't know her son didn't eat at the jewelry store because he was secretly seeing a girl. Gala performed her cooking duties splendidly for months until she started hearing rumors, which ruined everything.

"I'm not cooking for your mistress!" Gala shouted. As he was obviously attempting to deceive her, he had enough common sense to let it go and not put her in her place.

During those days, Ciprián and the Mexican met up at the port of San Juan once every few months to receive the merchandise, which arrived from Mexico in a container; they took a look at it before taking it to the gardening store. Usually it was his associate who told him when the container was coming, but one day he stopped calling. He only got a call from the port in which he was given a container number and a meeting time early in the morning.

Although it was an uncommon change in routine, he showed up at the port as instructed. When he reached the container, the Mexican wasn't there. However, he did stumble unexpectedly upon a familiar, but unwelcome face. It was the man of few words. He was patiently waiting for him with a cigarette in his hand, resting his back against the container.

"Well, look who it is! What are you doing here?" Ciprián said. Unbelievable! He thought he had left behind all traces of his old life. The Mexican never mentioned he was working with someone else.

"The Mexican was arrested at the port in Mexico," the man of few words said.

"How come? What happened?" Ciprián asked.

"He's not coming back," the man of few words said.

"It's all about the suspense with you, isn't it? Is there any other business I'm doing with you unknowingly? I don't want any more trouble!" Ciprián asked.

"No," the man of few words said. He threw his cigarette butt on the floor and squashed it with his foot, and then he turned his back on Ciprián and left.

Evidently, he wouldn't get much out of the man of few words. At first, Ciprián thought he would be murdered, that he really wasn't his associate but his enemy. After all, the last time he saw him was as a witness, watching him run after a Dominican illegal immigrant with a gun in his hand. It wasn't until he did some research that he found out that everything he had imported from Mexico wasn't only local art, but National Heritage. Recently, the government had begun to crack down on traffickers not unlike the Mexican. Then Ciprián realized that the Mayan god on his garden at home must have been taken from the premises of some pyramid in the middle of the jungle, or his muses taken from a colonial palace. Fortunately, nobody in Puerto Rico would come looking to expropriate Mexican artifacts.

Without Mexican art complementing his gardening products, the business could not differentiate from the rest, so Ciprián found a buyer and got rid of it. He had to think of something else to do to compensate for the business he had just lost. Since the jewelry store was leagues away from catering to upper class clientele, he could afford the luxury of diversifying his product offering even if what he offered not even remotely resembled a jewel. He emptied a corner of his store and called one of his second cousins. His cousin had a small business dedicated to distributing professional hair products for stylists. At first it was an experiment, but after he saw that people kept buying, he realized how much unexploited potential the business had. Ciprián soon convinced his cousin to sell him his distributing rights and became the sole distributor for the island.

Less than a block away from the jewelry store, he rented out a small warehouse for his products. If he forced them in, he could fit a container-full of shampoo bottles, conditioners, and dyes. He purchased four light trucks and hired four salesmen. They took orders and distributed products for sale and use by hair stylists, many of them excessively colorful and effeminate men running their own beauty salons.

On his way back home one evening, he found Irma affectionately saying goodbye to a man in front of the house. He had seen him before. It was her little boyfriend. Gala stood behind them, staring at them, smiling, waving him goodbye. Ciprián stopped his car and waited for the guy to leave the house before continuing to approach the house. Gala and Irma, who had been enjoying the moment just and instant before, became pallid and gloomy as soon as they saw Ciprián was home. They rushed into the house.

"I've told you not to bring that guy here!" Ciprián yelled.

After everything he had sacrificed to become a wealthy man and give a good life to his family, he wasn't about to let his daughter be with just any guy, with someone with no future. Being that there were so many opportunistic people out in the streets, he was concerned that the young man wasn't interested in his daughter, but in her inheritance.

"He's my boyfriend! You have to accept him!" Irma said, holding back her tears. She whimpered like a child.

Both Irma and Gala were blind. Her fool of a mother believed Irma when she told her all that nonsense of the love the young man felt for her, but was too naive to realize that weasel only wanted to make it to the top at her father's expense. To explain this fact to them would have been useless. Things needed to be dumbed down so they would get it.

"And you know well that you can't open your doors to any dumbass Irma decides to bring home!" Ciprián shouted, forcefully gripping Gala by her hair; he wanted to rip it off her head. "I've been telling you for a long time!"

Gala wasn't screaming. She only wept as she took on her husband's stinging smacks. Being pushed against the corner of the sofa, she tripped and fell on the floor.

"Leave her alone! Don't you dare hit her again!" Irma yelled. Although she didn't have the strength to stop him, she got in between him and her mother. He had never seen Irma pounce on him.

"Irma, get out of the way!" cried Gala, still on the floor trying to kick her way away from her husband. Ciprián struggled to get his daughter out of the way while his claws looked to grip his wife's legs and bring her toward him.

"We're grown up now and if you dare to hit her again, we're going to get together and hit you!" Irma yelled, in one single breath.

Her presumed display of bravery didn't last long, only until cowardice retook control of her body. When she looked at her father's face, she realized what she was saying and to whom. She fled, with him running behind her.

"You're saying you and who will do what to whom?" Ciprián asked, shouting. She ran down the stairs like a mad woman, stumbling with each step as she skipped and jumped her way down, slipping with loose bits and pieces of tile, stripping paint off the handrail to save herself from a deadly fall. Horror made her flee from her father as if running away from a homicidal maniac looking to eliminate her. She managed to lock herself in her car. "Come out of the car, Irma," he said without shouting at her to prove her he had calmed down. His daughter started the car. "Come out!" he yelled this time, giving hard blows to the hood and door of the car.

"No!" Irma cried, mortified and in tears. She shifted the gear to reverse and backed out of the house. Sparks came out of her rear bumper as she smacked it against the road as she went downhill.

She must have thought she had managed to escape a good beating, but it was him who let her get away. He wasn't going to beat her up, but he wanted to give her a good scare. But I knew that things couldn't go on like this. It was the first time that his daughter, daddy's little girl, stood up to him. She didn't go hide. She didn't keep quiet, watching what happened. She didn't get her panic attacks. She stood firm, albeit for only two seconds, but she did it. That day, when she stood between him and her mother to utter those words, he saw hatred in her eyes. Ciprián finally realized that physical blows to his wife became emotional blows to his children. So hard were these blows that now his children, grown up, would start rebelling against him.

At the time, Puerto Rico's Civil Code consisted of ten grounds for divorce. Of those ten, seven of them obviously didn't apply: separation, because he never separated from his family; insanity, because Gala was the only crazy one and she recovered within a week; the two related to prostitution, because he would never even consider asking this of any member of his family; abandonment, because he never left his family to fend for themselves; imprisonment, because the police had never caught him; impotence, because he had no doubt he was as strong as a bull.

The three remaining grounds perhaps shouldn't apply, but would certainly have been open to interpretation by a judge: cruel treatment, adultery, and habitual inebriation. There was no need to expose to a bunch of strangers the particularities of their life or the embarrassments they made each other go through. He didn't need to have people judge the choices he and Gala made throughout their lives, judge if they were at par with what was considered good and just as if morally qualified to reach such a determination. He didn't need anyone he knew to find out about so many minor details of his life, making judgment over his virtues as a businessman, being influenced to make or break business dealings with him or, even worse, spreading the word.

As if by divine intervention, the law of divorce by mutual consent came into effect that same year; it became ground number eleven. Excellent. Now they could just sign some papers and none of the intimate stuff would come to light.

Gala had no objection to the divorce, given Ciprián made her such a good offer. She would get to get to keep the mansion and get a hefty monthly allowance that would cover her expenses until she qualified for Social Security. In turn, he would get to keep his businesses. Child support didn't come into the discussion because all the kids were grown up. Case closed.

The last day in which Ciprián set foot on the house, Gala showed no emotion. He hadn't seen her act this way in years, not since the day when she came back from the mental hospital. When she looked at him, he couldn't tell whether she felt happy or sad. She seemed indifferent to the reality she was going through.

As he backed out of the garage, he took one last look at the house. As usual, Gala was sitting in the balcony, but that evening her house was dark and empty; loneliness was her companion. Ciprián rolled down the window of his car and waved her goodbye. Gala graciously returned the wave. After so many years of being together, they both knew they would never see each other again.

It would be his first night with Rita as a single man. Having a child and so many years together, I thought it would have been a night like any other. That wasn't the case. It was the first time he didn't feel the slightest remorse, given the double life he had lived until that day. No more hiding. No more lying. No more pretending.

The problem was that where he was heading to there wasn't love either. The difference between Gala and Rita was simply that he could stand Rita. Having never found true love, he settled for what he was able to get. Perhaps that's the definition of love. Settling for Rita, who loved him unconditionally, didn't seem to be a bad option. She made the first move, gave him all her attention, consoled him, and did everything to make him enjoy his time with her. That dedication made Ciprián care for the relationship enough to at least pretend to love Rita. That was enough for her.

At that moment, on his way back to his new home, he asked himself: What would he do with Rita now? Should he marry her after so many years of being his mistress and thus make official the farce of his so called love for her? Should he simply shack up with her, thus pretending to still live the adventure that was their love story?

I think both options were equally irrelevant. From a practical perspective, they were both old enough for nobody to really care if they married. But what would his relationship with his children be like if he got remarried?

Willie and Pey got along well with Quique, having been playmates as children. For them it wouldn't be so complicated. They knew Rita well; they trusted her as much as Ciprián did. They knew she had no ill will toward anyone. They knew she was simply a good woman who, as a young woman, let her heart choose; she chose things that although unpopular to society, were the right ones for her.

For Irma and Pablo it would be hard. They couldn't stand the sight of Rita. They would make her out to be a witch only interested in breaking up marriages. They would say Rita's family conspired to convince him that getting married was the best for both. They would say that Rita, since way back when she met Ciprián at the hospital, had a master plan: to live as a parasite for an entire lifetime until finally succeeding in taking over everything.

Married or not, his children would have to deal with the fact that Ciprián would no longer continue living with Gala. They would somehow need to find a way to meet, to see each other. He kept being their father and loved them as such. This is why they would need to learn to accept her as his wife, accept that he wanted to live with her, understand that he needed to move on with his life. They would need to understand that Gala would take no part in his future.

What would they do if they didn't manage to assimilate to the new reality and continued hating her? Would they not pay him a visit? Would he have to go visit or meet his children somewhere else by himself? Rita would have to keep living with the open wound of knowing she had so many people hating her and wishing her out of existence. She would be reminded of the fact every time Ciprián told her he was going visit his children and that she wasn't allowed to go with him. She would be reminded of the fact every time she answered the phone and some grandchild of his would ask to speak to his grandfather, knowing it was really one of Ciprián's children trying to get in touch with him. They would hate her enough not to speak to her over the phone.

What would be of birthdays, Christmases, and the rest of the holidays? Before, everything was easier. The family he lived with got all of the attention. That was the right thing to do. Would he now have to ridiculously split his time into his two families? What would it be like when he got old? Would his children stop seeing him as soon as he became unfit to get to them? Would they put aside their pride to see him, even with Rita at home?

His train of thought was suddenly interrupted when he reached Rita's house. The fragrance coming from the kitchen welcomed him. Beans were cooking, thus the aroma overtook the house. A celebration feast awaited him.

What he didn't imagine was that Rita wouldn't be there to welcome for him. Of her, only flesh and bones remained on the floor, amidst a cooking pot and two cups of rice.

CHAPTER XIX
Engaged pupil
Margarita's diary: July 31, 1982

I f only mom and dad were here to see me, they would be so proud! I know they remained so saddened by the breakup between Ángel and me. They would have been so happy to see me in love once again, but they gave up on that idea long before passing away. I'm old; even I had given up. At least God never gave up on me because he knows that love has no age. It was he who brought Ciprián to me and who struck our hearts with the arrows of love, hearts mistreated by the world, in bodies wrinkled by life.

The only one behaving like a jerk is my brother. He insists that I'm too old to take on another burden, as Ciprián is so many years older than me. From his condo in Florida, where he lives with his wife and children, he has the nerve to tell me what I need to be doing. This is despite the fact that I live alone in my own house in Puerto Rico; I don't have to answer to anyone. He says I need to think more about myself and my health, that I should consider moving in with him. Is he insane? I'm not going to live anywhere I can't call my own, where I have to ask for permission to do or say whatever I please! I'm not going anywhere near cold weather! No sir!

Well, that's precisely what I'm doing: thinking about myself and nobody else. He has no right to poke his finger into my business. It hurts me when he tells me these things as if he knows what was best for me. He knows nothing about Ciprián and how wonderful he makes me feel. I'm happy at his side. I've regained a part of myself, of my heart, a part that I had forgotten so long ago.

From the day he came to my home looking for a piano teacher, I knew he would be my last pupil. It was a miracle! He heard about me through the church because he was looking for something to keep his mind active. The poor man was widowed and he had just retired from work; he had some businesses before that he handed over to his children a while back. He could have chosen to do anything else but God guided him to me. That serves as proof of his limitless power. I'll keep lighting candles for the Great Power of God, like mom taught me to do, so that he keeps showering me with blessings. I want a happy and prosperous marriage.

Hence why I told father José María not to bring me more pupils for piano lessons. I want to put all my energy into spending time with my husband, to do things right. I can't afford to have any distractions.

It was evident that he had no talent for playing the piano. Old people always struggle to learn something new because they get thick-headed, thinking that they know everything just because they have lived for a long time. Ciprián was no exception. He would say that he didn't want to be corrected and would get angry when I repeated things more than once.

Naturally, he was wrong, but he would start staring at me with such an innocent smile on his face, knowing that he needed help, and waiting for me to stop looking at him as if I was going to tell him off. I found the whole ordeal distressingly cute.

Oh, and the stench! He smelled like a pine tree, as if he had bathed himself with Lestoil. It's a good smell to have emanating from floors and appliances, but from nothing else. He told me the perfume had been an old gift from his deceased wife, from the days they courted behind his ex-wife's back. He stopped using it when she passed away, but he decided to start using it again because he was coming to see me and wanted to impress me. He impressed me for sure. My nose, on the other hand, was not amused.

I wonder if the odor could have come from a mix of *botánica* ingredients. Having spent all of my life living with my mother taught me some things. My nose, which since I was a little girl took on purging baths made from all sorts of mixes, definitely hadn't lost its memory. My mother once told me of a potion that could be used as a perfume. It was given to a lover as a gift, but its true purpose was the total annulment of an already weak marriage.

I think that's what his mistress gave him, but it's of no consequence. That's something from his past. I wouldn't gain anything from knowing the details of his past marriages just as he wouldn't have anything to gain by revealing them. Would it make sense to start an argument with an old man and make him pay for everything he has done during his whole life? If he knew all I've been through, how would he react? That's why it's better not to ask about these things. I know him as the person he is today, not the person he was yesterday. I live in the present, not in the past. The past already passed and not even God can bring it back.

CHAPTER XX
$86 - 7 \neq 79$

Ciprián was lost. He drove at night, going block after block, hoping to stumble upon a road known to him. He looked for a familiar tree, an important building, anything that would let him remember the way home. But he had already driven those roads hundreds of times. The way was engraved in his memory. It should have been as simple as following the images, the memories I was sending him. After all, it had been that way all of his life!

Besides, they weren't just any memories. They all had important meanings. He needed to keep going straight until passing the restaurant where they sold that delicious chicken BBQ. He took Quique and Rita there for a late dinner the day they left Arecibo; she was deeply concerned and extremely nervous, by the way. Then he had to reach the main road, toward San Juan, driving past the lawyer's office that dealt with his divorce from Gala, the unsigned marriage to Rita, and all the paperwork needed after she died from a heart attack. He needed to turn right at the next traffic light, where his gardening business once thrived but that now had been replaced by a mall. From there, he had to keep going straight until reaching the port where he once received containers with cars, art, jewelry, beauty products, an airplane, and even the mysterious visit of the man of few words.

Instead of following the simple instructions I gave him, he distorted his memories and reached conclusions on which way to go. I couldn't understand what was happening to him. He drove past a place that looked just a teeny bit like his old jewelry store and, after looking at his surroundings, he figured he was lost around a Río Piedras made unrecognizable by the accelerated development of the country. Then, believing himself certain of where he was going, he went into a dark road that seemed to him like the one leading to where Gala lived. He used to venture there often, curious to see if her lights were on or not, although he never intended or wanted to see her. I didn't know the road he had taken. It was so strange to me that he would make such a mistake. He kept on turning left and right without listening to me or realizing how wrong he was. The more turns he insisted on taking, the more he got lost. The more he got lost, the deeper he got into a hole from which even I didn't know how to get out. I had never been there. I didn't know where we were.

With minutes turning into hours and seeing no evident signs of progress, Ciprián lost his patience. Desperate to get home, he decided to go faster, his logic telling him he could cover more ground in less time. He floored the gas pedal until the end of the block and, when he reached an intersection, burned rubber as he hit the breaks to a full stop. He leaned his head over the wheel like a mole and quickly looked side to side searching for clues to where he was. He smiled every time he believed he found a lead only to find himself again with no idea of the way out. That's what he did block after block, never realizing he was going in circles. During one of the periods where he was flooring it, he got blinded by red and blue lightbars followed by an annoying siren that kept screaming at him to stop.

"Shit," Ciprián said, as he slowed down toward the side of the road. He couldn't think of anything to tell the police. When he stopped, he watched them from the rearview mirror as they got out of the car. Something was wrong, something beyond a simple traffic violation. "Fuck! It's the PDP!"

Wait a minute. What? PDP? How did the Popular Democratic Party have anything to do with a cop stopping him for driving like a lunatic around a residential area? Of more importance, how was he able to take that memory from his brain without my permission?

An old conspiracy re-emerged, revealed many years back at his office in Arecibo by his cop friend. Ciprián saw the police as a threat to his freedom; the law had been following his footsteps for years until finally catching up to him. He was a fugitive lost at the wrong place and at the wrong time. Without thinking it further, he floored it, left the police car behind, and vanished among the labyrinth of dark roads.

Shortly after, his paranoia was gone. He had given me back the control of his memories in the same mysterious and sudden manner that he had taken it away. He was thirsty, so he stopped at a gasoline station to get something to drink. Great. Although we were still lost, a small rest from the shock we had just gone through didn't hurt. At that age, it was prudent to take care of oneself.

When he got out of the store with a bottle of water in his hand, he found two police cars surrounding his car and three officers pointing their guns at him.

He only got one phone call at the police station, but he had to figure out who to call. He couldn't call Margarita. She got tense every time anybody mentioned the police; she didn't like the topic. Besides, there was little she could do to help. She didn't know how to drive and, even if she miraculously knew considering all those years under voluntary house arrest, she surely would have had no clue about how to reach the station. No, calling her would only make her worried.

He couldn't call Gala's children either. Willie and Pey had moved to the United States some time back, so he couldn't count on them. He didn't want to disturb Pablo, who had work the following day. It wouldn't be fair to call him so late in the evening when he was in charge of all of the businesses Ciprián gave him after retiring. He didn't dare call Irma; she hadn't spoken to him since the divorce. I think the split hurt Irma more than Gala or me. It would have taken astronomically huge balls to call her just to get him out of jail. Maybe she would have been glad to hear such news.

"Hello? Who's this?" Quique said, raking his words. It was obvious that he had just woken up from a deep slumber.

"Quique, son, I'm sorry to wake you up," Ciprián said in a low voice, made shy by the shame he felt from having to call him from a police station.

"Dad? It's 12:30 in the morning. What are you doing up? Are you OK?" Quique asked.

"Yeah, I'm alright. Son, I need you to come pick me up at the police station," Ciprián said.

"The police station?" Quique shouted, and then cleared his throat. The news made his drowsiness disappear. "But, what happened? Which station are you at?"

"Nothing happened. I just got lost on the way home. The police stopped me just so that they could help me," Ciprián said with his eyes closed and two fingers between his nose and his forehead; he tried to extract the information he needed from his head. "I don't remember Margarita's address. That's why they brought me here," he added. The reality was that he wasn't sure about what exactly had happened. He refused to revisit how he ended up getting handcuffed by a cop and smashed against the hood of the police car for starting to yell and insult police officers. Something was wrong. It was ever more common to feel as if between him and me there was a loose wire. The noise in our communication signal was unsettling to me. "Hello, excuse me. Which station is this?" he asked the police officer, covering the telephone speaker with his hand.

"We are at the municipal precinct of Bayamón," the officer answered, visibly raising his eyebrows.

"We are at the municipal precinct of Bayamón," Ciprián said over the phone like a parrot, repeating every word the officer had said. If his son asked him how to get there, he wouldn't have had a clue.

"Bayamón?!" Quique shouted, in surprise. Since Ciprián had retired, he rarely ventured away from his home more than ten or fifteen minutes by car. "How did you end up there? How do I get to that station?"

"Give me one second. I'm going to get the officer to give you directions," Ciprián said, signaling the officer to come help him.

As the cop spoke with Quique over the phone, Ciprián gave a friendly nod to a man who looked at him from the waiting area. They had just spoken briefly as he looked for

Quique's phone number in his wallet. He had only compliments to offer at a photograph of Margarita, one that he likely saw over the corner of his eye inside the wallet. Their conversation was interrupted by the officer, who called Ciprián over to make his call.

When he came back to the waiting area, the man wasn't there anymore. The desk officers, who apparently didn't consider the privacy of their detainees of any importance, started discussing one of their cases in front of everybody.

"Check this out. We brought in this woman for possession and she called the guy who was just sitting there to pick her up," the cop said, pointing to the chair next to Ciprián's. The cop's audience, which was everyone sitting at the waiting area, followed his finger until all eyes fell on Ciprián.

"Which one do you mean? The fat guy with the Hector Lavoe sunglasses?" the other cop said.

"Ha, ha. No, the one with the red stain on his hand," said the cop. He scratched his hand in disgust, as if he had been the one with the birthmark. The cop was referring to the same guy with whom Ciprián had just chatted.

"Yeah, I remember. They just took him in. Why is he being questioned?" the other cop said.

"Listen to this. He was sitting there all harmless but when we checked out his record, the son of a bitch had dozens of pages of offences listed," the cop said, and he looked to the sides, adding suspense to the gossip. He wanted to leave the bet for last. "Domestic violence and sexual assault, baby! Ha, ha!" he said out loud, striking his knuckles against the desk between each word and closing with an applause.

That man sitting next to Ciprián? It's true that appearances can be deceiving.

Ciprián's quarrel with the police won him a trip to the psychiatrist. Margarita, given the conditional liberty she had granted herself early on in her childhood, allowed herself to leave her home to visit the doctor. Doctors didn't make house calls, as father José María did.

"Well, Ciprián, you answered most of the questions correctly," the doctor said, as he wrote all the secrets he would save for Margarita and Quique. "But you had a bit of a hard time recalling those three words I told you to remember. You missed one. Then, when I asked you to subtract by 7's, starting from 100, you missed the correct number four times," he added. The doctor kept staring at Ciprián. The doctor seemed to be looking for a sign that Ciprián remembered those long minutes in which he guessed, failed, and laughed at his own ignorance and mental disconnection. Ciprián remained quiet and thoughtful, resting his chin on his hand, smiling at those who were waiting for his reaction.

"What does that mean? Will he get better?" Margarita asked, holding her husband by the hand.

"It may just be something common that comes with age, but there's also a risk of developing some type of dementia, like Alzheimer's disease. It's too early to diagnose," the doctor replied as he wrote up a prescription. "For now, Ciprián, I'll have you do some lab tests. We're going to have to follow up every couple of months to see if there's any improvement," he said, handing him a paper full of the scribbles they taught him how to make in medicine school.

Ciprián, as expected, wasn't paying attention. He was distracted by the waterfalls of sweat dropping from his doctor's forehead. Despite the Siberian cold inside the air-conditioned office, the doctor was sweating like a pig.

"Everything will be alright, honey," Ciprián said. Seeing that Quique, Margarita, and the doctor were all watching him, waiting for him to react to news that he didn't even hear, again he decided to pretend he had understood. He kept quiet but, to appease Margarita, he held her hand firmly and gave it a loving kiss.

He knew that regardless of what the doctor said, he was in good hands with his wife. At that moment, he wasn't aware of the fact that Margarita would save him from many hardships as an old man, sooner than he ever imagined. Besides, he got re-married to avoid such hardships as being alone, handicapped without a caretaker, depending on his children, living in a house he couldn't call his own, and— God forbid—ending up segregated to a retirement home. He married Margarita so that she could care for him with all her love and dedication until the last days of his life.

He was old when Rita passed away, too old to get into the headaches that a new relationship entailed. He didn't need to love; he didn't need to look for another wife. However, life as a retired man gave us much to think about loneliness. He needed a woman who was tolerable enough, capable enough, and with a big enough heart to never leave him when he needed her most. What Margarita didn't know was that, even if Ciprián came to love her as a wife more than he loved the other two, he could have easily ended up with any other woman; he just happened to meet her first. His relationship with Margarita started out of convenience and then turned into love. Romantic, isn't it?

CHAPTER XXI
The house wins
Margarita's diary: January 21, 1962

First, I checked out the slot machines. I didn't find them very interesting. The room was filled with old people mesmerized by the senseless music coming out of the machines, conned by the miserable alms they won, gluing their arms to the reel handles so they wouldn't stop. They would keep playing for the rest of the night, driven by pure illusion, hopeful that the next pulling of the handle would get them the big prize.

Then I checked out the card games. People seemed to be a bit more refined there, like they knew what they were doing. They played Poker and Blackjack. I can't understand those card games for the life of me. I don't know the rules. I don't know how much each card is worth, and I can't count. I don't know how to bet, not to mention any of the strategies used to win. Cards are not for me.

Finally, I came across the game of roulette. There was a pretty handsome guy there who had just won a lot of chips. I sat next to him to see if I could learn something. He put almost all his winnings on those little squares with numbers.

On each number he would place two, three, four, and up to ten chips in different colors. He was so fast. He knew what he was doing. Sometimes he put chips between two squares. I didn't get that part. All I know is that the ball always landed on a number where he had bet some chips. Each time, he won more and more chips. He was unstoppable.

All of a sudden, he stopped. He grabbed all of his chips and switched tables. That must have been one of his strategies. Maybe he got more luck that way. I couldn't keep watching and learning from where I was sitting. Without him, I had no other business sitting at the table so I slowly stood up, went to the restroom, and came back. Once again, I sat next to him.

I still hadn't built up the courage to talk to him. He had a veil of mystery around him that intrigued me. I wanted to ask him to teach me how to play like him but I'm too much of a shy girl. I was hoping that sitting next to him he would take the initiative and would try approaching me. I gave him some discreet and friendly smiles but he never even looked back at me. He remained serious, concentrated on his game. He knew what he wanted and he wouldn't let himself be distracted by a simple girl like me.

He said something into the ear of the guy turning the roulette, like a secret he didn't want anyone else on the table to know about. As soon as he was done with his chat, the ball stopped. Again, a winning number. Were they cheating? It didn't surprise me then how much money he won.

I tried keeping a closer eye on what was going on, watching attentively both the dealer behind the table and that handsome player to see if I could figure out their trick. Maybe he was changing the ball, or somehow made it coincide with the wheel on a specific number, or they managed to distract all the players at the table while chips jumped from a losing square to a winning one.

Whatever they were doing, they were good at it. I never managed to figure it out. Two big security guards came to kick me out of the casino. They were saying I was disturbing customers. I didn't even speak to anyone! There was something going on at the table. I'm not stupid. They must have seen me trying to figure out their trick and thought I would tell on them. That wasn't my intention at all, far from it. I went to the casino to learn something new and have an adventure. I only wanted to learn, not to get into any trouble.

The casino has been just one of the many disheartening experiences I've had with the world. I can't leave my home without someone coming to stick their noses into what's none of their business. Someone always has to stare, judge, and make all sorts of insulting comments: how I walk, what I wear, the makeup I use. They pay attention to these things as if they were of importance to them.

Just a few days ago all I had to do was to walk into a clothing store and look at myself in the mirror for two seconds, and I was already falling victim to people's attacks:

«Madam, why have you come here so terribly dressed? Your clothes are torn and stained all over. You're not at home. This is a public establishment. Have you no shame?»

«Why do you even bother trying to fix up that mess you call hair? Do you believe you have any chance of becoming beautiful? I'm so embarrassed for you!»

«Who are you smiling at, yourself? Do you really believe you still got it? What are you looking for? Are you looking to get engaged again to someone who can't stand you to the point of turning queer? »

The values of my dear Puerto Rico are no more. People have no decency and plenty of cruelty in them. Disrespectful, they are.

Not even when I go to mass at church, can I get some peace with God. There's no reason why anyone should care about how much money I put into the collection of alms basket. If in some stranger's opinion I put too much or too little that's my problem, not his. I give to God and to the poor what I can. They also don't have any reason to question why I'm taking the communion, making themselves out to be the most saintly or pure. Besides, how is it their business that I'm too fat or too skinny? Is that an intriguing enough topic to desecrate the sanctity of mass?

The purpose of going to church should be to ask God for forgiveness, to worship him, to aspire to become a better person and earn a place in heaven. Those who criticize the most are the ones who pray the most, who go into the confession room the most, who believe they are the most worthy of God's blessings, but inside and outside church, they disregard his teachings. What they do is harm their neighbor not by accident, but willingly. It's the supposed exemplary followers of the faith who laugh the most, who stare the most, who judge the most, and gossip behind my back.

I feel hounded, as if the world had put a plastic bag over my head just waiting until I run out of air and suffocate. If taunts and insults from random assholes on the street is all I'm going to get, then I'd rather stay home. I won't go out. I feel at ease here and have everything I need. I can sit comfortably and relax; I can entertain myself by listening to the radio or by watching TV; I can cook; I can take care of mom, who's getting pretty old now. If there's someone who really needs me, who truly wants to come and see me, let him come. No. There's only hatred to be found outside. The world, if things keep going the way they're going, will soon come to an end. May God have mercy on us all!

At least I've still got mom around to help me and keep me company. She's still healthy despite her years, thank God. Since dad's death, she's been spending her time exchanging letters with my aunt in New York, whom she always called by the name of *'la comay'*. The letters help keep family ties to give support to one another. She also lost her husband recently, although she didn't take long to re-marry.

His new husband is a divorced man in his fifties. He's from Arecibo. She openly says that she didn't get married out of love. She sees love as something impossible to get, something reserved for young people, who are more open to believing such fantasies. She married out of convenience. As a seamstress of dresses and women's underwear at a clothing factory, she wasn't earning enough to live a decent life alone. She felt she didn't have a steady job, that she could be fired from there at a moment's notice. Her husband gets a good income buying cars and exporting them to a partner here in Puerto Rico. They can live well off both incomes with enough stability to get them through tough times.

It's not as if she only married him for his money. For her, the most important thing is that they can both get along together and live happily. He seems like he really cares for her, treats her well and with respect. She often gets a little something from him to keep the romance going. Although she says that getting small gifts is simple romantic nonsense, she doesn't complain.

She feels fortunate that he's not a man of bad habits, which is what many Puerto Ricans turn into after finding themselves aroused by so many exotic things around them. He doesn't do drugs and rarely drinks. He stays away from those who approach him with vices. He says that those are the people who get you in trouble by pressuring you into getting hooked or getting you into fights that they brought on themselves. According to him, evil comes at you quicker when you're already surrounded by evil. That's why he's always with trusted friends who don't pressure him into anything; they know him too well already.

When mom reads my aunt's stories about her new husband, she lives and delights in them as if she was right there with her. Nevertheless, when it comes to getting another husband she says fantasizing about it is enough, that dad was and will be the only man in her life. She says she has everything she needs and that she has no urge to take on another man who might not suit her, who would bring his bad habits, and who would start telling her what to do or where to go. A new husband would certainly have her take care of him when he was no longer able to do it for himself. She would have to clean up his shit until he died. It's unavoidable because women always live longer than men.

In the last letter she sent, my aunt couldn't stop praising mom's witch-like powers. Mom had given her a detailed account about how she had managed to transport her spirit into my aunt's house in the Bronx. She highlighted the mess of books, magazines, papers, desks, old fans, chairs, old clothes, toolboxes, car spares, jelly jars filled with screws and nails, and many other things in a room that she called 'the room of horrors'.

She classified as 'horrid' the yellow wallpaper with red flowers and blue stripes over the living room walls, but she was moved when she saw two puppies run happily from the living room into the kitchen. She did, however, warn them about the stench that was taking over the whole house. Lying on the floor under the sofa, they had pieces of newspaper soaking in urine as part of their puppies' training, but they hadn't noticed that urine had also been curing itself in between the sofa cushions.

Her biggest discovery was that of an extremely rare picture, never before seen by her, in which she appeared with dad and my ghost uncle in front of the San Cristobal castle. What was odd wasn't whom she was with, nor what was behind them, but the fact that it was taken during the one and only day the world would see her as a blonde with straight hair. Dad wasn't fond of dyed hair. He said he had married her because she was beautiful with a natural look, and that she didn't need to put any crap on her hair to look better.

What hurts us the most about dad's passing was that it happened before it should have, because he didn't want to take care of himself. He never went to a doctor. He never even mentioned to anyone he was feeling ill until it was already too late. We were taken by surprise the day we had to rush him to the hospital.

He complained of strong pains in the abdomen that weren't letting him walk. Naturally, the first thing we thought was that he was just full of gases, nothing more. However, the nurse discovered, tucked inside his underwear like a tampon during a woman's period, a bunch of toilet paper over-flowing in blood. Although dad denied confessing to us for how long he had hidden his disease, the nurse assured us that the amount of blood she found could only have come out after months of progression.

Just as quickly as we were made aware of his condition, I lost my dad. No warning, no goodbye.

I never really thought about the impact this would have in me during the rest of my life. I had no time. I had lost the most important man in my life but I was immersed in funeral arrangements and organizing the week of rosaries for the deceased. Mom was devastated. She, who had always been in charge of everything, spent those days distracted in silence. She couldn't help in anything. My brother, the man of the house, offered me no help either.

On the second evening of the rosary week, I was able to better understand what was happening. I was preparing some snacks, *mezcla* sandwiches. I had readied the Spam, the cheese, and the mayonnaise to go into the blender, but I was still missing a can of red peppers to complete the mix. Mom was standing in the dining room looking out the window. I tried asking her to help me find the can but still no change; she was mute.

I got the feeling that something was up, something that went beyond the depression that had taken her over. I got closer to her and touched her back. She took a few seconds to react but then she looked at me and smiled. She pointed her finger at some clouds in the distance, still uttering no words. I wasn't sure what she wanted me to see, what she wanted me to look for. She knew. To her, it was evident and incredible. She took my arm and shook me violently as if she didn't want to let me miss something so wonderful, but I never managed to see what she saw.

At that moment, after almost a week of remaining silent, she became herself again. Once she calmed down, she told me that she had just seen the Great Power of God over the clouds. The divine presence blinked his eyes and stared directly into hers with infinite love. For her, that apparition was proof of the greatness of God; it was a sign that dad was in good hands, a sign that it was time to recover her strength and to never stop believing in God. That apparition filled her with faith.

CHAPTER XXII
Memory ~~of~~ a wreck

S weetie, I spoke with Simón this afternoon and he told me that the Cash & Carry had closed down," Ciprián said, as if he still couldn't believe the news. He said it in the same way he had said it a decade back, when Simón decided to sell the business to a big supermarket chain so that he could enjoy his retirement.

"What is he doing now?" Margarita asked. She knew that Simón had retired after closing the sale and was now looking after Ciprián's parents. That was her way of torturing herself. Sometimes she got the right answer, sometimes she didn't. Perhaps that gave her some hope that her husband might still be somewhere there, that she wasn't losing him.

"It's a relief for me to find out that it closed, you know?" Ciprián said. He continued to talk about whatever was in his head as if he was talking to himself, ignoring Margarita. "When I moved out of Arecibo and left him the Cash & Carry, I kept a copy of the keys to the warehouse. You know, by mistake. After that day, every time I went back to Arecibo I would forget them here," he said, but then paused and looked at Margarita, searching for signs that she understood the gravity of the situation. She seemed to have no clue of what he was talking about. "It was something that I had always on my mind, a great worry," he added, intertwining the fingers of both hands and gently shaking them back and forth, thanking God for having removed such a large load off his back. "There was only one set of keys! If Simón somehow lost his keys, he would have been in trouble."

"My God, yes! Thank God nothing happened," Margarita said. She was pretending. She got used to acting in order to keep Ciprián calm. She knew that arguing with him and correcting him every time he said something that made no apparent sense would only confuse him and stress her.

"I had that in my head bugging me and guess who called today?" Ciprián asked.

"You told me Simón called, didn't you?" Margarita said, with confusion in her eyebrows.

"Exactly! He told me that the Cash & Carry had been closed down," Ciprián said. This time he said it lowering his voice, as if it were gossip. When he told me that, it was like taking a huge load off my back! I kept the keys to the warehouse when I moved out of Arecibo," he said, again looking into Margarita's eyes for signs of worry given such news.

"Oh, my! What if Simón had lost his copy? He had only one, right?" Margarita asked, acting as if extremely worried. What the heck? Humoring him still was the best option.

"Ha, ha, ha. That's what I was thinking! All of a sudden, Simón calls me on the phone as if I had called him with my mind," he said, pausing some seconds, and then continued to discuss the topic in a very serious manner. "Look. I told him that if he needed the key, I could give it back to him. I don't need it. It's not my business anymore," he said, wiping his hands clean of the situation. "But, see sweetie, the feeling of relief I got when he told me the warehouse closed down!"

"Oh, dear! Look at the time!" Margarita said, looking at her wristwatch. That was her way of steering away the conversation before it turned into a broken record. Changing the topic on him made him lose his train of thought, but at least saved Margarita from endless repetition. "Can you go with Paty to the market? She should be here soon. We need bread, eggs, and milk."

"Yes, well. Let me see if I've got any money," Ciprián said. He reached into his back pocket and took out his wallet. It was packed with handyman business cards, which he added to his collection whenever he walked by a hardware store in case he needed to fix up something around the house. They were mixed up with a pile of receipts accumulated over months. "I'm broke. Only have three dollars left."

"No, dear, you don't need any money. Remember that I pay Paty at the end of the month," Margarita said.

Paty had been shopping for the family for more than twenty years, ever since Margarita turned into a recluse. Why did she become a recluse? I never found out. When Ciprián met her, things seemed normal. She always had an excuse not to go out. She preferred to invite him over for dinner and that he spend time with her at home. Whenever he brought up the topic, she simply said she wasn't interested in leaving the house and that she felt at ease there. She said it uncomfortably enough for him not to talk about it anymore. Ciprián didn't care; he could still go outside as he pleased.

My theory is that it had something to do with the strange altar she had set up in a room at the back of the house. It consisted of a small wooden house for a life-sized bust statue of Jesus Christ. He was wearing his crown of thorns, with blood flowing down his forehead and a visage of eternal suffering looking up toward the sky. Margarita had put a large black rosary around its neck. The cross had its own figurine of a crucified Jesus Christ encrusted in it, and rested hanging over the edge of a glass container filled with water in front of the statue.

There were big candles around the statue: red, white, yellow, green, and many other colors. The candles depicted the images of the saints or angels for which each flame would burn. There were also statuettes no bigger than six inches scattered around the altar: one of the Virgin Mary, one of Saint Barbara, one of Saint Francis of Assisi, and one of a man wearing a black suit with a hat. Next to the group of statuettes there was an eighteen karat gold ring with the face of a tribal chief, his head covered in feathers. According to Margarita, it was her father's wedding ring.

She promised her mother she would take care of the altar. According to Margarita, her mother was a fortune teller. What I don't understand I can neither accept it nor refuse as truth, especially when a trusted person like Margarita tells it to me, having witnessed her mother's powers. Nevertheless, Ciprián, whose family didn't believe in such things, would get the heeby jeebies whenever he went inside that room, especially at night. He avoided it even when his condition worsened and he stopped being himself. Wandering around the house, he would get to that room and the bad vibes would make him turn around and go the opposite way. Only God knew if spiritism and *santería* had been the things keeping his poor wife stuck within the confines of her home.

190

Coming back to Paty, she was a single woman in her forties when Ciprián moved into Margarita's house. He always remembered her wearing those tight jeans with black sneakers and shirts that, given her overwhelming weight, must have required a lot of effort to be tucked into her belt. She had short hair; no hair was longer than half an inch. She covered it up with a baseball cap. The money and the grocery list were squeezed inside her belt bag, among other things. Although reserved, she was a very responsible woman, which is why Ciprián knew little more about her, only enough to judge her.

"Is Paty the lesbian?" Ciprián said, with a mischievous smile. At any point in life, the strongest memories are generally the filthiest. Normally, he would have kept that sort thinking quiet, but given his condition, he had no limitations; he said what he thought.

"Don't be rude. She's only manly. That doesn't mean that she likes women. Here. Finish eating, so that you can go. She'll be here any time now," Margarita said, feeding him his last spoonful. She stood up and cleaned up the table.

"Sweetie, where is it we're going now?" Ciprián asked. It rubbed him the wrong way that, at the last minute and without being kept in the loop, she made plans to go out.

"You're going to the market with Paty. Remember: bread, eggs, and milk," Margarita said.

"Well, I don't know. Let me see how much money I have on me," Ciprián said, grudgingly. Once again, he reached for his wallet and opened it. He rummaged through all the papers he had inside, counting his dollars. "I have three dollars left. How many do you think I need?"

"Paty will be paying for it, dear," Margarita said from the kitchen as she washed the dishes, with a tone that hovered over the limits of patience.

"OK, OK, my love," Ciprián said. From one moment to the next, he found himself sitting at an empty table. His wife, busy in the kitchen, was making a ruckus with pots and pans. "Hey, sweetie, when is lunch going to be ready?"

Thus his confusion kept developing until becoming permanent, a state of never-ending doubt that kept him wondering how he fit into his surroundings. He got lost in thought, desperately trying to make sense of it all. It was an impossible task. He lost track of what he looked for all on his own. He made circles around his own thoughts without realizing that hours went by without him ever getting any-where. He tried to live a normal life but had no way of knowing that his ties to me were all but broken. I could do little more than to watch and wait until I got the random chance to manage his memories again. This way, at least, he could have a few seconds of peace.

As the years went by, he began to be haunted by the terrify-ing images of the charred bodies that once tried escaping from his burning Cherokee. But this wasn't just any night-mare. Just like what is imagined or the ideas one has, night-mares are created by combining memories of real things or things that come from the imagination. They are composed of known things, things with which one has already made peace. One way or the other, a normal person is prepared to visualize the crudest vision the head is able to come up with. However, with Ciprián slipping from my hands, that process stopped working.

In this case, he was no longer recalling the ghosts from his past, those that he had left behind. His problem lay in the fact that those terribly vivid memories from his younger days weren't his anymore; he didn't recognize them as such. Ciprián, in his condition, slept on his bed with his mind as clean as that of a child. He had no means to prepare for the unexpected, to imagine the unimaginable. He had no means to foresee the upset of having such a gruesome film downloaded into his brain without warning.

A child completely carbonized. Eyes, ears, mouth, and nose indiscernible one from the other, hair consumed by the flames. Sulfur, the rotten smell of sulfur. Suddenly, the creature began to cry. He was alive! Ciprián made his way among the smoke to take him in his arms, the remaining skin on the child's body slipping from Ciprián's hands and dropping on the floor of the plane. The cries of that unrecognizable human intensified. Ciprián tried to calm him down like he did for his children: rocking him, singing to him, but he wouldn't stop crying. Affection would not heal his wounds.

For a moment, he looked at the black man burning on fire. The horror in his eyes was still there despite him being already dead. A bloody piece of glass went through his neck. He could see himself reflected on the glass, an image of a much younger and care-free Ciprián, much calmer than he was, barely troubled by the chaos around him.

"Ciprián!" cried the black man he had given up for dead.

Terror made him jump from his bed and wake up abruptly against the floor. The walls of Margarita's house, the bed, the windows, nothing was familiar to him. He didn't know where he was or how he had gotten there. How could he recover from the impact of a nightmare if after waking up

he didn't even find himself at his home, like any other normal person would?

He was alone in the shadows, covered in sweat with his
heart in his hand about to explode. The door to his room,
his only escapeway, was shut and he couldn't open it. He
feared being imprisoned and drugged by some psychopath
who, any moment, could come back to do whatever he
wanted with him. He tried to force the knob open and
banged the door with all his might only to get distressed as
he faced failure, resting his head against it and kneeling on
the floor out of frustration.

"Ciprián? Do you need to use the toilet, dear?" Margarita asked. She had no other choice but to lock him up in his
room at night. It was for his protection. She knew that the
darkness of night confused him and made him wander
around the house, although she surely couldn't have imagined what he was actually going through.

"Yes," Ciprián said. He had forgotten the reason for his
panic. He had forgotten the nightmare he just had and the
psychopath who was keeping him imprisoned. He had forgotten this many times before and would forget again in the
future, with or without Margarita coming to his rescue. The
fear, the anguish, the confusion—in the end, boiled down to
having an urge to pee.

"Come, let's go. Don't piss all over the toilet seat, for
the love of God!" Margarita said.

CHAPTER XXIII
Timely exit
Margarita's diary: September 29, 1961

I 've been a witness to mom making her *riegos* and *mejunjes* ever since I can recall; I was a little girl when I started getting cramps in my hand during spelling tests and couldn't finish them. She cured them. She knows how to protect people and drive away hateful spirits. However, to my surprise, she's equally adept at black magic.

The head of a poor chicken rolled, decapitated at my mother's hands. Ángel would never have imagined that his name would be written in pencil on a brown piece of paper and stuffed into a chicken bled dry as part of a spiritist ritual. Likewise, he would have never thought that the woman who would have been his mother in law would put that dead chicken inside a paper bag, light it on fire, and throw it out over a four-way street. This was the same crossing used so many years ago to protect me from the man in the penguin suit sitting on the living room sofa.

I comfort myself knowing that at least Ángel told me the truth. He manned up and told me he couldn't marry me; he had to leave. He couldn't keep pretending to be happy by my

195

side. He didn't want to ruin my life. He didn't want us to live unhappy, miserable, and sorry for having chosen to spend our lives together. He didn't feel capable of bringing children to this world and raising them under the illusion of a happy marriage. He didn't feel he could ever look at me with the loving eyes I deserved.

Mom didn't buy the story. For her, it was bullshit. She assured me that nancy-boy, his new nickname, wouldn't be able to harm me again. She was convinced that Ángel made up the whole thing so that he could run away with another girl. I don't think he was lying. He doesn't have it in him. He's never lied to me and there's no reason why he should do it now. If he tells me that he's finally found himself and that he prefers men over women, then I believe him.

My brother, on the other hand, didn't seem to be surprised at all. He always considered Ángel to be too effeminate, from the high-pitched buzz that fluted its way out of his mouth, to the exaggerated mannerisms that complemented his twisted wrists. I remember being told about his peculiar ways, but I disregarded such comments. Over time, my brother must have seen that our relationship was getting serious and decided not to bring it up again. To be honest, I could never tell his manly side from his effeminate side. To me he was gallant man, an elegant man, a full-blown man.

Evidently, my eyes are blind to those things.

He says he'll feel more at ease in New York. Given the state of our country these days, he would end up left for dead in a ditch if the wrong people found out about his condition. He would have to spend the rest of his life as an outcast, taken in only by people with his same disease. With any luck, pretending to be straight would let him keep his job because, otherwise, not even the church would take pity on him.

It's not like he'll be welcomed with open arms by the United States. My aunt lives there and says that despite the fact that we get our citizenship as soon as we're born, *gringos* treat Puerto Ricans as poorly as they treat blacks. That's what awaits Ángel, man-lover or not. What plays in his favor is that it's such a big city! He tells me around eight million people live there. With that many people, he can live in peace and find himself a lover with whom he can live without scandals. No one needs to be questioning or criticizing what he does or doesn't do. No one needs to be gossiping about the details of his personal life. No one needs to care.

I'm not sure if mom's spell made me stronger or if I was simply less hurt from being dumped for a man rather than a woman, but I'm proud of myself. I suffered greatly. I trembled and wept as bad as when I was at the hospital. I was so scared of falling back into that terrible state, but I held on. I resisted. I didn't let my thoughts take over again.

Dad tells me I need to find the positive side of things, think about all of the opportunities that this change in my life could bring, and think about how to re-invent myself. He says that the human being is the only animal with the power of language; because we have that power, we are able to organize things in our heads and have bigger and more complex thoughts. According to him, having those bigger and more complex thoughts influences our daily habits. These habits, apparently, are tied to the way I think. They're simply habits and they're not necessarily there to do me good.

Was that his way of telling me that I'm fat? Maybe he's thinking of the bigger portions I've been serving myself at dinner recently and all that candy I've been munching for dessert. It's true that I do look a bit plumper when I stand in front of the mirror, but there's nothing better than mom's cooking. Did he choose his words with care and put them in such a metaphorical context only because he didn't want to hurt my feelings?

He tells me that if I want to change something about myself, I need to be aware of what I think and find the positive side to any of my negative thoughts. My habits will automatically change and will behave in accordance to those positive thoughts. The more I practice, the better, because although it's true that thoughts influence habits, it's equally true that habits influence thoughts. As I keep improving my habits these will, in turn, reward me with more positive experiences. Going through more positive experiences will facilitate my positive thinking. It's like a feedback loop.

Brilliant. It was his quasi-intellectual way of telling me to watch what I eat. I need to figure out whether the cravings my body gets come from needing food or from simple gluttony. As I keep the habit of listening to my own body, it will start asking me to indulge less until getting me back to my normal weight and keeping it stable. I grinned. I don't care about that. However, if he put the effort to handle the topic as delicately as he did, it's because he worries about me. I know that dad is always watching out for my wellbeing.

He told me to trust him because what he says is fact, not made up. That way of thinking was what raised him from the abyss and has brought him many more blessings. He assures me it was the path he followed to transcend and become a god; I would never reach enlightenment until I reflected seriously on his words and acted.

A god?

Before I could react to such incredible news, he took out a copy of 'Bristol's Almanac Illustrated' from his pocket. He got it as a gift a few years back when he was grocery shopping. The first random page he opened that day was titled 'Socorro', which happens to be our family name. The almanac had illustrated a family composed of six: three males and three females. There was a father, a mother, a son, a daughter, and two strangers. It couldn't have been a coincidence. It had to be a sign, a forecast of what was in store for our family. When dad saw the illustration, he knew that those two strangers would become our future family members.

My brother got married last year, adding another girl to the cast. Only one was left. Until a few days ago, it seemed that Ángel would have been the one taking on the role. He's not the one, but that doesn't mean that the almanac is wrong. At least I know I have nothing to worry about. Soon I'll meet the right man, just as the great Bristol predicted.

Since the day I spoke with dad, I've been thinking. I think his words make sense at a different level, one much less superficial than the one he intended. He only wants to see me get skinnier and more attractive so I can get another guy to marry me before I get too old and become a spinster. I want to look beyond the limits of my body. I want to think that perhaps there's a way to change what I want to change about who I am, to change my soul.

It's not easy to ignore how the life I was forming for me and my family has fallen into pieces. I had a plan. I was going to get married, have children, and become a professional pianist. Now what? How should I be expected to begin thinking positively? Is there some sort of gadget I can use to crank out good habits?

Everything vanished before my eyes as if it had never happened. The only remnant left, the proof that I was ever engaged, is that stupid matrimonial drawing we had made of ourselves by a professional artist. I looked so beautiful with my hair worn up and he looked so handsome with his new haircut. I had it all within my grasp and I lost it. I lack the will to start again from scratch.

Mom does what she can to console me as I spend my nights kneeling in front of the toilet with my swollen head resting against the basin, screaming my throat dry and bathing my face in tears. She gives me a lot of water, cleans up my face, freshens up my neck, and massages my back and my cramped arms. When she hugs me, I really feel the love she has for me. She wraps me in her arms and doesn't let me go during my bursts of rage, during the tantrums in which I curse and damn God, his Son, the Holy Spirit, and the Virgin Mary. I demand answers. I beg him to bring my fiancé back to me just as he was when we first kissed. I offer my life to him, my devotion, and my sacrifice; I'd give anything to be in his arms once again, to return to what ceased to be.

Enough!

How could there possibly be a positive side to any of that? Is there anything positive about feeling exhausted? Or about having such a heavy chest and not being able to breathe? Or about being pinched all over my body, feeling the fierce pecking of a vulture feasting on my back, my lungs, and my heart?

Thick-headed is my name. I can't manage to convince myself of my absurd tricks. I'm me. Trying to behave like somebody I'm not is the same as lying to myself. I prefer being alone and cast aside rather than to pretend that the ensemble of the terrible and painful things I've gone through is not as terrible as I made it out to be. Let's be realistic. It is what it is. Period.

Of course I would love to think positively! I would love to get the demon that pesters me off my back, anguish. I would love to be blind again, unaware of the truth. I would love to go back to dreaming about the life I had ahead of me, get lost among those thoughts rather than fight against them. To dream about the things to come is so much better than to unsuccessfully cry out to what is vile within, begone!

I spill what is left of my heart out on these sheets of paper, even as tears cloud my sight. Ink is running away from my words. They are crying too.

Stress

M ind and sight both betrayed Ciprián. It wasn't the usual type of betrayal that had to do with blurry memories or the aches and pains of old age; it was more than that.

"Do you know who I am? What's my name?" a strangely familiar voice asked Ciprián.

The size of her eyes, the roundness of her face, the length of her extremities, in fact, any attribute of his only daughter morphed subtly by the second. Slide by slide, a film projected in front of his eyes that showed him a variety of possible mutations and realities that made his daughter appear to be a stranger.

Even Ciprián had stopped managing his memories. The norm since birth was to see reality, interpret it with existing memories, and then react to it. That job had been slowly taken away from me by Ciprián these last few years, many months before the doctor who sweats like a pig diagnosed him with Alzheimer's. Although he did a terrible job at it, at least he followed the norm of reality-memories-action. However, now it didn't even seem certain that his hands were on the wheel. His mind and sight conspired against us. They wanted to change the norm. They wanted to begin by a memory and then see how they could make it fit into reality. They didn't care how much the change distorted reality. They didn't care that whatever Ciprián saw, I saw as well, so I would be lost with him, struggling to regain my orientation and make sense of my surroundings.

I couldn't give up. I had to be ready as soon as he needed me, as soon as things went back to the way they were before. I could go back to being a part of his life, to the time when he could do anything. Why else would I be here?

In addition to the gravity of his state, soon he would completely lose his voice. He needed long pauses to think, inhale, and take advantage of the exhalation to spit out words from his hoarse, worn out throat.

Who are you? It was such a simple question.

"You are... Celín's little girl," Ciprián replied timidly. He was guessing, of course, poorly.

"No dad," Irma said, disappointed. "I'm your daughter! Irma!" she said slowly, loudly, and with exaggerated intonation, treating him as if he was deaf rather than demented.

"You're Irma... my little girl?" Ciprián replied, incredulous. "Look at how pretty you are!" he added, while he tried to adjust his belt, which kept his short trousers up to the level of his belly-button.

"Who is this slacker? Do you know him?" Irma said, putting her hand on her brother's back to appease him. It must have been hard to take the hit of not being recognized by her father. "Here. I'm going to help you," she said, loosening up his belt and tucking his wife-beater onto his trousers along with the white shirt he wore over it.

"Tighten it well. Otherwise, my pants will fall down," Ciprián said, smiling.

"Take a good look. Who does he look like?" Irma asked.

"My sonny boy... Pablito," Ciprián said, again guessing. This time he was right. Dumb luck.

"Very good, dad! Very good! This is Pablo! Your son!" Irma said, and then she lowered her voice and addressed her brother. "Give him a hug," she told him. Of his five children, he was the least affectionate.

"Dad, where is Margarita?" Pey said. Like the rest of his brothers, he knew that putting his father's memory to the test was a waste of time. Ciprián was all but lost. However, he wanted to spend time with his father, whom he only saw twice a year when he came to visit from the United States. He didn't care much that there were not many other topics they could talk about together.

"Margarita... was taken yesterday night," Ciprián said.

With respect to the news he had just announced, no clue. He, as messed up as he was, had to rummage into his memories and see what he got. I was barely connected to him at all. Whatever impact I could have had in a fraction of a second of lucidity was miniscule. Regardless of how much effort I put into it, two was all it took seconds for him to forget whatever I showed him. Why beat my head against the wall? I just had to relax and enjoy the show.

"You don't say? Who took her?" Pey asked. They also had no idea what he was referring to. Margarita was in the kitchen talking with Willie while she prepared a jar of lemonade for her visitors. She wanted to be a good host to her step-children. No one had taken her anywhere.

"He came on a large airplane... a man... came down from the skies and took her," Ciprián said. When he finished, he stared into Pey's eyes with a smile locked into place.

Pey smiled back; it was the forced smile of his youngest child who, when hearing the nonsense coming out of his sick and senile father's mouth, struggled to pretend everything was OK. Pey didn't want to confuse him or make him not feel at ease. I saw how much pity he felt for his father and how helpless he felt toward him. On the other hand, what Ciprián saw was just the smile of a stranger interested in spending time with him, and that made him happy.

"Look who it is! Margarita came back from her travels!" Pey said, playing his role well. He exaggerated his gestures and pointed toward Margarita, pretending to be surprised at finding someone who had been lost.

Ciprián got very excited when he saw her, this time being taken to him by Pey's hand. He squelched the brown grocery store slippers he wore over his thin, black moccasin socks. Clearly, he wasn't sure who that woman was. Likewise, he remembered nothing of her being taken away by a man on an airplane. However, he had no doubt about the importance of that woman to him. She had to be important if everyone around him was behaving like she was.

"Here you go," Margarita said, as she handed Pey a glass of lemonade.

"Thank you Margarita," Pey said, but he kept looking at her, trying to decipher the faces she was making at him. She seemed to be trying to ask whether Pablo or Irma wanted something to drink. Ciprián's two eldest children sat down on the sofa as soon as Margarita made her appearance and avoided crossing eyes with her. Still, she must have seen how disdain consumed them from the inside out. "No. Don't worry. Thank you Margarita," he answered.

Pablo and Irma behaved a bit different than Willie and Pey. Both of them being adults with families and grown children, rather than using Rita's death as an excuse to rid themselves of resentment and hatred, they accused Margarita of manipulating and taking advantage of their father. They claimed that although Ciprián's condition hadn't been diagnosed at the time, it must have affected his judgment. They said she took the opportunity to con him into marrying her with the intention of getting all his money.

At all moments, Pablo and Irma's visits had to be mediated by Willie or Pey because Ciprián's two resentful children refused to have any contact with Margarita. They didn't want to have to see her or talk to her, even to the point of not accepting the fresh lemonade she always prepared for them in good faith—she already knew they wouldn't accept it—hoping they would change their mind. Margarita so understood the situation that, being master of her home, she was willing to go through the humiliation of relegating herself to the kitchen. This was the most elegant solution Willie and Pey could come up with so that Pablo and Irma could share the same four walls with Margarita and not rip her head off.

Ciprián, who with his condition at such an advanced state didn't even recognize the people in front of him as his children, had long before rid himself of any emotional burden related to dealing with the hatred aimed at any wife other than Gala. However, it wasn't always like that. A healthier Ciprián would have never allowed Margarita to be disrespected in such a way. Since he married Margarita, it was he who went by Pablo and Irma's house because he knew that otherwise, he would never see them. Even after the day when the police found him lost in Bayamón and he saw the doctor for the first time, he had to be the one making arrangements so that his children would, at least, come pick him up and take them to their house for a while.

However, the moment in which his children finally deigned to go into Margarita's home to visit him didn't come because time had softened their hearts; it didn't come because they saw how much of a good and well intentioned woman she happened to be. The moment came simply because they realized their father had become too weak to take car trips at his children's whim.

Adding Quique into the equation implied another set of visiting rules. If Pablo and Irma didn't want to see Margarita, they definitely didn't even want to smell Quique. Because his job was near the house and, almost daily, he went there for lunch, Margarita had to advise him not to visit in an effort to keep harmony and avoid conflict.

In his own way, Quique was in charge of cheering up his step-mother. He arrived to the house in a happy and energetic mood, as if hoping his strength would stick to her.

"This situation may seem pretty hard for us now, but we have to take it with a bit of humor. We have to laugh it out," Quique said, dipping a spoon into some cheese flan, his father's dessert. "We can't let ourselves get depressed by those who don't deserve our attention."

"Yeah," Margarita said, unconvinced.

"Margarita, they don't come here to talk to you, or to ask you how you're doing, or to help you out around the house! Months can go by and they don't even visit their own father! I can understand Willie and Pey because they aren't living here, but the other two have no excuse," Quique said.

"I'd love to be a strong as you are. I try. I really do try but I can't," Margarita said.

"Look. If we let them, they'll bury us before Alzheimer's buries dad. Right, Chepo? Ahm! How delicious!" Quique said, as the spoonful of flan fell effortlessly into Ciprián's willing mouth. Food tasted like cardboard to him, but he still had a bit of taste for sweets. "Veeeery good! One more!"

Although the moral support Quique offered to Margarita was very important to her, he wasn't really aware of the load Ciprián put on her shoulders, how consumed he had her. The constant among those around her—including those who hated her—was that after a few hours of chats and games with Ciprián, they all went back to the comfort of their homes and left him alone with her.

It wasn't all about taking on the hatred coming from Ciprián's ingrate children. Margarita was also the one in charge of doing the dirty work, that of keeping him alive: to cook for him, knowing well that sometimes he wouldn't accept her food and she would have to cook something else; to keep track of his medicine, knowing well that if she didn't watch him, he would spit it out and hide it because he didn't feel sick; to keep him clean, which also meant cleaning up after him.

It was Margarita, not his children, the one fortunate enough to find a yellow pond next to a lamp in the living room corner, left behind by her husband to cheer up her morning. Margarita had to clean up the trails of shit Ciprián left around the house because he couldn't hold it; he got lost between his room and the bathroom. Eventually he used diapers, but who had to wipe his ass and change those dirty diapers like a mother would do to her son? His wife was in charge of that.

Margarita had to get inside the shower with Ciprián, knowing that he was scared of water and could pose a danger to her. He was a man and still had some strength left in him. Ciprián would look at the spurt, then at Margarita, and would alternate between the two while dilating his pupils, breathing heavily until finally attempting a wet and naked escape. She had to gather strength from her old arm muscles, in pain due to her arthritis, to keep him in his place and give him a shower.

She took that on herself with all the patience in the world. She asked for nothing in return. The love that captivated her when he was himself, not a living corpse, was her calling. She was an angel. However, how could she survive without a compliment from him? How to survive without a tender caress? I can understand that the love she felt for him when they got married was strong, enough to withstand the loneliness she must have felt after losing the essence of what had once been Ciprián. However, is a platonic love really enough? What about physical love? What about affection, hugs, kisses, and everything else that made them feel alive as they shared their vulnerability? Perhaps she didn't doubt the plenitude of her sentimental love for Ciprián, but she couldn't deny the latent lack of physical love. Love cannot be called love if it has missing parts!

This must have been the main reason why, on various occasions, Ciprián found his sleep disturbed by the Margarita's old hips rocking on top of him. The lateral bars of the bed, originally installed as a response to the repeated falls he suffered after his nightmares, screeched as they were fiercely shaken from side to side. Margarita, squatting over her husband, struggled to keep her balance. Very considerate of him, she was. She didn't want to hurt her sick husband.

"You're quiet," Margarita said, whispering to his ear. "Do you like it?"

Ciprián didn't have the strength to show his affection toward that woman who seemed to be enjoying so much being on top of him. He looked at her eyes, trying to figure out who she was, but he remained quiet, still, emotionless.

"Ciprián, say something, honey!" Margarita shouted at him, kissing his lips, his forehead, his eyes, his ears, anything to get a reaction from his husband.

"Rita, I... have a surprise for you," Ciprián finally replied. The lateral bars of the bed ceased their noise. Margarita didn't move. "I already spoke... with the lawyer... to sign... the divorce papers."

Margarita laid her head over Ciprián's chest and, shortly after, let him feel her tears drop. She struggled to breathe between each whimper. Ciprián, worried about that woman suffering at his side, caressed her hair. Upon feeling his touch, Margarita couldn't stand the pain and suffering that made her heart beat so strongly. She let out her agony as anyone with a broken heart would, with a scream.

CHAPTER XXV
No shoes, no freedom
Margarita's diary: December 17, 1953

W hen it was time to eat, the guard knocked on the door two times and then opened a small service hatch at the bottom. That was the only chance I got to feel a ray of light. If I positioned myself in front of the hatch like a crocodile—chin, elbows, knees, and ankles hugging the floor at the same time—I could take a good look at the pair of white shoes that brought me food. Normally, there were three guards watching over me: a man with big fat feet, which he lazily dragged over the floor and whose rumbling could be felt from a mile away; a newbie with brand new shoes clumsily trying out key after key until he could find the one that opened the hatch; a woman who, with her small feet and her delicate manners, was difficult to hear coming, showed up at my cell unexpectedly, and gave me no time to get into position to greet her shoes.

The hatch was my only portal to the external world, accessible for only five seconds, three times per day. For the guards, its sole purpose was to slide through there a stainless steel tray that was designed to last forever at the hands of prisoners with a lifetime sentence. I was served breakfast, lunch, and dinner in a ruckus as the tray banged the edges of the hatch, the same way pots and pans do as they slip away from soapy hands. The shrieking and scratching as it ran across the floor, in and out of the cave, gave me an unpleasantly coarse sensation within my teeth and gums.

Blinded by darkness, I would look for the spoon, carelessly thrown into a random deposit by an inconsiderate fool who didn't care to think that there might be someone trying to find utensils. Evidently that person wasn't part of the cooking staff, because my days of freedom taught me that the people serving the food keep a strict discipline and rigorous order of things.

I liked eating my food following a specific order, which was not an easy task considering I couldn't see what I was putting in my mouth. Luckily, the military discipline followed by the cooking staff made things easier. The first thing I needed to do was to touch the back of the tray with my hands. That way I could feel the relief of the pressed metal, the size of each different deposit, and then position it with the larger of the two middle deposits facing toward me.

The upper right end of the tray was reserved for the dessert, which could consist of pineapple slices, pears, peaches, apple purée, or mixed fruits. I always ate the dessert first because it was the sweetest thing on the tray, especially that delicious nectar that came along with the fruits. It cheered me up, except for those damned days when they chose to serve papaya candy. I can't understand how after preparing them with so much sugar, vanilla notes, and cinnamon—as delicious as those ingredients are on their own—such an aberration of nature could be created. People waste so many well-intentioned hours of their life preparing that dish, delighting some whose sense of taste I sincerely put into question, but to me serving as the most efficient vomit inducer ever invented.

Mixed vegetables, located at the upper left corner, followed dessert. Vegetables are hard to mess up. The cooking staff maintained a stable offering of steamed corn, green beans, peas, and carrots.

While I finished my vegetables, I would dip my nose into the deposits closest to me and see what I had as a main course. Beans were on the left: white, pink, or red, each broth unmistakable from the other. I mixed them with the white rice in the middle deposit and with either the beef, chicken, or pork chops at the right corner deposit. If they didn't serve rice, then they served mashed potatoes or spaghetti noodles with meatballs.

I have to say that whenever I got the mashed potatoes, I wouldn't eat them because I always had to rush to the toilet. I had to leave what I was eating and run before I soiled myself. Then I ended up with such a strong stomach upset that I wasn't hungry anymore. On the rare occasions I was able to continue eating, the size of the room was so small and the stench so dense that even bread tasted funny as it touched my lips. It was better to avoid eating, if I could. Besides, it was disgusting for me, given those conditions, to lick my fingers after eating those yummy smoked pork chops.

The water was in the upper middle deposit. It was good for me not only because it helped me digest my food, but because it relieved my dry throat. I spent my days screaming. Otherwise, they would have surely forgotten about me. My mom always said: «The squeaky wheel gets the oil. »

What did I do? Did I do something wrong? Why am I here? I wouldn't get tired of shouting questions at them, but I never got any answers back. They always ignored me. My only interaction with the outside world was through the hatch that brought me food. It was the sole way to console myself as I was filled with doubt, knowing neither my captor's intentions nor their willingness to cater to my needs.

It's just that I didn't even know why I was there. It was simply unfair for me to be locked up when I hadn't harmed anyone. After all, it was he who came looking for me. They should have taken him away instead of me and leave him to rot in that hole. I was just minding my own business, sitting quietly in the hallway until I heard his malevolent little voice asking me to come closer to him and help him out.

He called me, whispering from the door of his room, sticking his head out and looking left and right to make sure nobody was coming. I was alone. I was the only one who heard him. I had seen him before in the game room. He was so skinny and cute, like a little brother. He had sky blue cotton pants on, very soft, and was used to walking around shirtless.

He kept calling me with the palm of his hand, which was almost entirely covered by a giant red birthmark. He snapped his fingers, calling me like a dog. I asked what he wanted but I didn't raise my voice. I was curious and I didn't want to get him into any trouble, not before I was able to find out what all the mystery was about. He signaled me to come quickly before someone saw me, and said he had something very important to show me, some secret he had hidden.

When I got close enough to the door, he grabbed me with his little hands and guided me inside. He quickly closed

214

it and skipped childishly until reaching his night stand. From the bottom drawer, he took out something wrapped in a mess of ribbons and pieces of newspaper. He tore out the ribbon and the newspaper pieces in excitement, just like any kid would when opening his Christmas gifts.

He soon unveiled the secret; it was a snow globe with sparkling stars falling over a smiling half-moon. The child put the globe in my hands and grabbed a small key it had on the bottom. When he turned it, it played a familiar tone: «*lullaby, and good night, with roses bedight…*». He told me that music helped him sleep and that it may be of use to me during my sleepless nights. I didn't know what he was talking about. I never suffered from insomnia here, but I found it cute that he worried about me. According to him, I'm weird because many people here have problems getting a good night's sleep.

Seeing I had no use for his cure against insomnia, he took the snow globe and placed it carefully over the night stand. He took my hands and stroked his forehead with them, letting my fingers fall softly over his eyes and his mouth until resting his cheeks in between them. After a few seconds, he held my wrists and kept sliding my hands over his chest. I felt the ups and downs of his ribs and his heartbeat spike up.

I wasn't getting what his intentions were. I felt my hands being tugged down until they were hidden below his sky blue trousers. I was speechless. It didn't even occur to me to say no, or scream, or run away. I tried stopping him. I struggled. I resisted. I shook my hands violently with my fists closed, but he didn't let go. He didn't give in. He held a firm grip on me to stop me from shaking. He managed to loosen my fingers one by one until I couldn't keep them closed any longer. I lost my strength given the pain I felt and had him—who made good use of his window of opportunity—snuggling between my hands.

He begged me, asking me to stop struggling and let him move freely over my body. He was persistent, the kid. He really wanted it and he wouldn't give it up so easily. I had no idea what I was doing. I saw myself from another plane of existence where morality was unknown and nothing was written in stone. During the struggle, the only thing I felt from within was flattery. I found the amount of interest in me fascinating, filled with so much raw desire. His persistence was wood to the fire that consumed me. I felt desired, so I wanted to return him the favor.

It took me by surprise how well-endowed he was! He also knew how to hold me, how to kiss me, how to move, how to take my clothes off before I could even take notice. He knew how to do so many things I hadn't learned to do. He made me feel like such a fool for everything I was missing out on in life. I couldn't conceive how a child could make me feel better than every grown man did before him.

I didn't notice when the light turned on. I was mesmerized with the whole of my body on top of him, both of us lying on the floor in a hypnotic trance. It wasn't until I was tugged back by two hairy gorillas dressed in white that I came to be aware of my surroundings. I fought to stay in place, wrapping my legs around the child, but he was so light that he was raised in the air along with me. They held me firmly and shook me fiercely, trying to untangle him from my legs until they finally uncoupled me. I was taken away kicking and screaming. They locked up in the dark room.

I sang; I whistled; I became adept at making animal sounds: the growl of a lion, the trumpeting of an elephant, the squawk of a parrot, and the song of the *coquí*. I just had to silence the voice inside my head yelling at me, telling me that I wasn't good enough, that I was useless, that I couldn't even accomplish the simple task of running away from my family and being independent, that I would live forever as a parasite, and that I was a waste of a human being. I wept. Tears came out of my eyes because I knew none of it made any sense but I couldn't do anything about it. I buried my fingers deep inside my ears and continued humming songs, growling, singing, whatever it took to quiet down the voice. I kept going louder and louder.

All of a sudden, I would hear the white shoes coming. I soon realized that their coming was the only constant that brought me peace instead of torture. I waited for them day by day. They were like sunrises that brought to me light and life. The brightness they brought allowed me to escape from those four walls and transport myself to a parallel version of the world, a world where I had absolute freedom to do what I wanted, where people were good and everybody loved me.

It was in that world where I made friends with the members of the symphony orchestra, whom I met during one of my strolls around the park while they were rehearsing. It was a pleasure for me to be with them those first few days, sitting on first row seats. I woke up to the flawless interpretation of Mozart's 'The Marriage of Figaro', a perfect energy booster for mornings. The feel of the vibrations resounding in my body gave me the willpower to do it all. Blood flowed through my veins. I was filled with excitement and hope.

217

After so many happy days, I stopped feeling tortured by nights, which were transformed into gala evenings. While the symphony rested, the pianist came and offered a concert on a grand piano with exquisite interpretations of Liszt's 'La Campanella' and 'Hungarian Rhapsody No. 2'. I sneaked out of the theater to lie on the grass, where I could enjoy the concert but also admire the beauty of the starry night. I looked for constellations and counted each and every star I saw in the sky, hoping to be lucky enough to see a shooting star that would grant me a wish before I fell asleep.

My only request, night after night, was not to have to leave, to be able to bathe myself in music forever. I loved the orchestra. I didn't want to wait so long before I could hear them again. They pandered to my wishes and stayed for longer, interpreting all my favorites: Rachmaninoff, Tchaikovski, Chopin, Mozart, Liszt, Schumann, Brahms; they even let me conduct them with an imaginary baton!

I didn't know what I was asking for. The orchestra ended up being a double-edged sword. At one point they came and never left. At first it was a blessing and a dream, but then it became a nightmare. While it was true that they were playing my favorite pieces, being surrounded by a symphony orchestra twenty-four hours a day was torture.

I felt an unbearable stomach ache that came and went as the orchestra squeezed my entrails. Regardless of the position of my body—lying down, standing, squatting, on my side, on my head—the stinging pain didn't leave my gut. The orchestra, previously composed of sweet elderly people, now scorned at me and attempted to snap my eardrums in unison. I could neither sleep nor remain awake. I felt dizzy and my body was exhausted. I lost consciousness.

I woke up; I'm not sure how much time after. I felt fat raindrops pinching me, torrential rains falling senselessly from within the dark room. I smiled because the symphony orchestra was gone, the voice in my head was no more, and even the rainfall poured noiselessly. Content with being able to find myself again, I took my clothes off and began to dance under the rain.

Naked and soaking wet, I saw as, all of a sudden, the door that had kept me locked in that damned dark room was unlocked. I had only to look outside and there I found them, the white shoes worn by the nurse with small feet and delicate manners. I never doubted that the shoes would come and set me free from a world imagined by me, and would give me my life back.

The red-haired nurse was plumper than I had imagined. There aren't many red-haired girls around anymore. Thrilled, I hugged her and let her know I was ready to leave.

CHAPTER XXVI
Like the good old days

Margarita looked into Ciprián's eyes hoping she would find somewhere him hidden inside his head. At times she would stare so deeply into them that I was almost convinced she could see me. She did it only to torment herself. She knew he would never be able to talk to her, to return her the love she gave him. She must have felt enraged with whoever created this world for exiling her husband from his mind until his body gave up. The worst for her must have been just having him so close, enough to touch him, and be teased by a man who ignored the existence of his loving wife, a man forbidden to her. Why punish her so? What could she have done to deserve such penance? Didn't it suffice to punish only him?

Or perhaps she asked herself, how does it feel to be trapped there? What could he be thinking about? Perhaps she was hoping he could at least hear her words, even if it was impossible for him to react to them. Maybe she wasn't capable of believing that a person could lose himself inside his body. Could she have been so naive as to think Ciprián would have one day awakened from the spell that stripped him from his being? Could she have thought that he would come back to living a happy life with her? Perhaps. Her frustration could have given her plenty to think about.

In any case, the truth was that Ciprián left her alone. She was alone with a human being incapable of hugging and kissing her as he did before, with a human being incapable of consoling her during tough times, of celebrating the great times, of caressing her, of whispering to her ear, "I love you". She was alone with a human being for whom she had sacrificed so much of herself and had wept endless tears with no hope of being returned the slightest affection. How could it be possible to live happily loving someone without ever being loved back?

Ciprián didn't care about nor took care of any of that. He was too busy wandering from room to room, taking baby steps. He would amuse himself discovering new worlds within old pictures he found scattered all over the house. In them, he found family and friends he didn't know he really knew, on occasions staring at them with great interest for a number of minutes. Some days, Margarita would sit with him to look at them and would tell him who each one of those strangers in the pictures were, but although Ciprián was capable of showing surprise and was pleased to hear about his family, he would forget it within the next minute. It was a moment of temporary amusement, more than anything else.

He also amused himself with the ceramic and porcelain figurines Margarita had collected throughout her life. Just like a child, he was attracted by their design and colors. When he saw an interesting one, he picked it up and took it everywhere with him. When he found the perfect place for it, he simply left it there over desks and dressers in different rooms. It was then Margarita's job to spend part of her day looking for them and restoring them to their rightful places, at the same time senselessly reprimanding her sick husband. It is worth mentioning that the room that housed an altar with saints and candles was the exception; Ciprián never went there.

If he saw a paper out of place, he would grab it, fold in half, and put it back where he found it. However, Margarita didn't have many papers scattered around the house. Most of the papers he found were letters from religious organizations and private non-profits that—as was the case for many willing elderly with disposable money in their pockets—asked for donations to fund hundreds of supposed goodwill activities for the poor in the third-world. She never had the heart to say no to them, so she diligently answered each and every letter, attaching her monthly donation.

One day, as he went on his exploration route, Ciprián halted for a few seconds in front of the living room mirror. What he saw was surreal. He didn't see a Ciprián decayed by his illness and his age, but a Ciprián during his better years. He looked young, strong, and able. He had a whole life ahead of him. However, he found himself a stranger in a house that evidently wasn't his own. He figured he was there for a reason, looking for something. He heard a noise. It came from outside, on the porch. He heard people talking and laughing.

"Take care, my dear. I'll see you tomorrow," Gala said. It was Gala!

Ciprián was confused. What was his wife doing inside a stranger's house? Who owned that house? Who was Gala speaking to? From the living room, he quietly rushed to the window that looked out to the porch to spy on her.

There she was. It was a beautiful Gala, a happy Gala before children or infidelity. She hugged dearly what was a stranger to Ciprián, kissing his cheek. That man was an intruder to his marriage. He was enraged by his discovery. She was mocking him and he couldn't let her get away with it.

As soon as the man took his paws away from her, he came out to the porch and confronted her. He wasn't about to do it with words; he would unleash his wrath upon her. He didn't care about the consequences, what the neighbors would say, what the police would say. They would call it a crime of passion. They would see it as what a broken heart was willing to do for a woman he believed to know and love, but who ended up being another street whore. Society would protect him.

Gala was caught unaware, too busy watching her lover walking away from the scene of the crime to see her husband coming. Ciprián gripped her hair and buried his claws into her head.

"Nah, nah, nah, nah, nah, nah, nah!" Ciprián shouted with the incomprehensible stutter that had taken over his speech months back.

He didn't give her a chance to explain or defend herself. He wouldn't give way to an unnecessary trial. He had caught her red handed. What she did wasn't open for interpretation. He began beating her against the iron bars that enclosed the porch without ceasing until he saw blood come out of her head. He wanted to make sure he would leave a scar to remind her of her treachery.

"Ciprián! What are you doing? I don't understand!" Gala said, crying and yelling from where she lay on the ground.

"Nah, nah, nah, nah, nah, nah, nah!" Ciprián said, boiling with rage. He went back inside to look for a revolver he would have kept inside the closet decades back, one that he obviously wouldn't be able to find because it didn't exist. He was in the wrong house and in the wrong year.

When he went back into the living room, he saw one of Margarita's figurines on top of the table. It was that of a farmer girl with a bandana on her head and two geese by her side. He held it in his hands, inspecting it with curiosity. All of a sudden, he heard weeping in the distance. Someone was in trouble: a woman. When he made his way out to the porch, he found Margarita lying on the floor whimpering with a bleeding wound on her forehead. Horrified by what he saw, he rushed at his clockwork toy pace to help her.

"Nah, nah, nah, nah, nah, nah, nah!" Ciprián desperately called to Quique, who was already unlocking the gate but struggled doing so because of his shaky hands.

"Quique! Get him away from me, please! I don't know what's happening to him!" Margarita screamed.

I had never seen her behave like that, so petrified by her own husband.

It was so painful to bear witness to such injustice! Why did Margarita have to pay for Ciprián's past? Why did it have to be her, when she had been such a good woman to him? Why did my hands have to be tied during that precise moment? I would have been able to prevent such a painful tragedy. I would have been able to do something to stop him, to dispel him from that illusion. It was stupid to believe he was re-living his past, to believe Gala could have been so daring as to let herself be seen in public with her lover. I would have been able to snap him back into reality. It was only a goodbye, a farewell between Margarita and his son.

The next morning, Quique came by the house. It wasn't time for lunch yet; he came earlier than usual.

"Margarita? Are you there?" Quique asked, after knocking on the kitchen door. He tried turning the knob but the door had been locked from the inside. He knocked a bit harder, thinking that the TV was too loud for her to hear him, but there was no response. He went looking for her in every room but he didn't find her. She had to be inside there. "Margarita!" he repeated. His knocks turned into punches. "Margarita! Are you OK?" he said, as his nerves started to overtake him. He knew something was wrong. He began striking his body against the door but he couldn't break it open. "Stay here, dad."

A short while afterwards, his son came back with a crowbar. He nailed it between the door and the frame. After three good pulls, he stripped the lock open. Despite having unlocked it, he still had to force his way in kicking the door until he was able to unstick a wet towel that lay between the door and the floor.

"Oh my God! Margarita? Margarita!" Quique yelled from inside the kitchen. Ciprián heard him from the hallway. After a few seconds, his son shot out into the living room.

While Quique was on the phone, Ciprián peeked into the kitchen through the door and walked inside as he normally did during his daily wandering. On the floor there was a bucket with dirty water and a mop resting on top of the squeezing basket. The kitchen countertop top was filled with fruits and vegetables, cheese and margarine, eggs, meats defrosting, ice trays full of melted ice, juice cartons, milk, water, and other packaged products. The fridge, impeccably clean inside, was empty. Pots and pans occupied the four burners of the stove. She had cooked a beef stew in the pressure cooker, white rice in a pot, beans in a casserole, and fried ripe plantains, called *amarillos*, on the pan. The stove burners were still set to the max but no fire burned; they must have been left burning the entire night until the two gas tanks were completely emptied out.

Finally, he found Margarita sitting on one of the breakfast table chairs with a cold half-finished food serving on the table, watching her black and white TV while serenely resting her bandaged head against the wall. I imagine that, after she sealed the doors and windows with wet towels and she turned on the stove burners to the max, she didn't think it would take long before the fire consumed all the oxygen. Finding herself bored of waiting, she must have decided to keep herself busy cleaning and cooking the rest of the night.

Ciprián remained there for a bit watching that woman sleeping comfortably in the kitchen. He then turned back and continued to explore the house, as usual. He would never see her again, not in life, not in memories.

CHAPTER XVII

Margarita's diary

D uring some secret meeting, Ciprián's children unanimously came to the convenient conclusion that sending their father to a retirement home was the best for him. They only needed to find the right place, which they did. Given all the comforts it offered, it was easy for them to become convinced that he would need nothing else, that he would be more comfortable and happy than at the care of any of them. Surely they had a clean conscience. When taking the decision, they must have thought about their father's wellbeing and not of the load that whoever got to take care of him would take on. Thousands of dollars were paid every month for him to live in that small paradise. Only the best for dear dad.

To be frank, the retirement home was pretty well equipped. It was one of those complexes lost in the countryside, surrounded by fresh air, nature, and birds that sang. It was the ideal setting for the elderly to get a sneak peak at what they would find when they went up to heaven, or wherever their final destination was. There was security and controlled access around the clock, professional nurses giving the best care, and spotless facilities. Tenants could walk around stone paths that led to well-groomed gardens with flowers and orchids, and to relaxing water streams that fell from small fountains made of wood and Chinese stone for their delight.

For those strong in faith, there was a statue of the Virgin Mary resting inside her little house made of cement, protected by glass and surrounded by flowers. For those who still had it in them, there were entertainment centers with TV's and games. For those with a working sense of taste, there were excellent homemade meals. The administrators energetically announced to Ciprián's children how lucky they were since just that week a vacancy had opened up, which meant that some other guy had just died and there was nobody else waitlisted to join the home. What an honor!

To my surprise, the experience of being sent to a retirement home was different to the depressive monotony I expected to experience. For Ciprián, every minute wandering around the common area was full of constantly changing emotions. One minute he could find himself in the middle of a party, scavenging the territory of strangers to find a good group to join or someone interesting to meet. Another minute he could find that, thanks to the new norm his body set to make his memories fit into reality and so distort it at will, strangers turned into friends and family. The next minute he could find himself sitting alone in peace, just people-watching. In the worst case, he could find himself afraid, lost, and confused in a place he wasn't familiar with. However, these feelings were random; the next minute he could easily forget everything and start over. Ciprián could feel the same levels of happiness and sadness that any healthy person could and, likewise, all would depend on his environment. The main difference was that once that moment was gone, he would forget it while, for a mentally healthy person, forgetting was much more difficult.

That difference, although it seemed trivial, was of great importance to be able to deal with his condition without him constantly falling into depression because of not knowing who or where he was. Other elderly, said to be healthier, had their own demons to deal with. Ciprián didn't have to be consumed by the bitterness inside the man in the wheelchair; he only opened his mouth to curse at nurses, rudely knocking over his food tray to the floor. Neither did he have to be as foolish as that woman who put so much makeup on and dressed up in her best clothes day after day only to spend her days sitting in front of the TV. She would be the first one to get up when someone came. Surely she felt a tickle between her legs every time she heard the front door opening up because she knew somebody had a visitor.

Unlike them and many others at the retirement home, Ciprián didn't have all the baggage made up of an entire life filled with hate, worries, or depressive desires. There was little of that life accessible from his brain. If there was little to be worried about, surely there was little to suffer from.

Those with intact memories were destined to suffer the most, not Ciprián. The root of all suffering grows not from the shocking moment lived as much as it does from the memory that makes it stick. The memory grows, intertwining with others equally arduous, gaining strength until consuming he who bears them if he cannot make peace with them. On the other hand, he who can forget cannot suffer.

Once a month, a group of church ladies would come to visit. Despite them being in their fifties or sixties, they were warmly welcomed by the retirees. They brought airs of youth to people desperate to revive their days of glory. The ladies sat with them and listened to their stories, those of their lives and families, their pain and grieving. They brought food, sweets, and church songs to get them to sing and dance.

One of the volunteers noticed there was an old woman struggling with herself to sit, so she came up to her and offered her help.

"No. Don't help her. She can do it herself. The thing is that she's been getting too lazy with age. If she starts getting too much attention now and everybody starts doing everything for her, she'll get even lazier," said an old man standing next to her.

"So, are you her caregiver?" the church lady said.

"Hah! Of course! We've been together for fifty-nine years. She was my sweetheart for four years and my wife for fifty-five. That day we got married I swore to be there for her until one of us passed. Well, neither of us has passed, but even if I'm ready to go she still needs me, so here I am," the old man said.

"Wow! Fifty-nine years together! And you look so well!" the church lady said as she gave him a slice of cake on a disposable plate. "Tell me, how long have you been living at this place?"

"It's been almost one year and a half already. I feel fine, considering my age, you know, but my wife keeps getting worse and she needs to be cared for well," the old man said and paused for a few seconds, as if recalling the same discussion he had thousands of times in the past and reaffirming his decision. "I told my children. I don't want us to be an unnecessary burden for anyone."

"Oh, but don't you want to spend time with your children and grandchildren? To be there for them? I'm sure they would love to have you home," the church lady said.

"Let me tell you something, my dear. I had my father living at my house for five years until he died," the old man said, looking at her like a naive dreamer. "I saw him fade away at the hands of this damned Alzheimer's disease and now he's killing my wife too. I don't want this for my children. Whatever good times I'll have with them will never compensate for the bad. Of that, I'm sure."

"Oh! May God bless you! I will keep you in my prayers," the church lady said, her mouth covered, and then put her hands together as tears almost fell from her eyes.

Ciprián, who was innocently savoring his delicious ice cream but not the vanilla cone, broke the tension by handing the church lady an empty cone deformed by the lick of his tongue. After doing so, he wiped his hands clean with the bottom of his shirt and kept on walking. The flashing of the TV screen caught his eye, so he got to the entertainment room and sat to watch it.

"I have three grown daughters already, married and with children," an old woman said, sitting next to Ciprián. She was always yapping about her children, be it at Ciprián or at the wind. Before Ciprián sat there she was alone. She must have scared away all the church ladies because she just wouldn't shut up. "My husband wanted at least one son, you know, so that his last name would remain in the family. God decided to give us only daughters, each of them a blessing," she said, pausing for a moment. Ciprián was watching cartoons on the TV. Suddenly he felt a poke alerting him that the conversation continued. "Oh, they are great. Professionals. The eldest works as an engineer at the Energy Authority. She completed her studies at Mayagüez. The middle child is a real-estate agent. The youngest is a university professor at UPR. She was a 4.0 student at an all-girl's high school. She always said she wanted to be a doctor and she even got accepted into medical school but I always knew she would change her mind. I didn't see her as a doctor," she said with the certainty of a clairvoyant. "Six grandchildren they have given me: four girls and two boys. What do you think? More girls! And what is yet to come! I'm waiting for one of them to get me some great grandchildren!" she said, raising her voice. "She is twenty-nine years old and she still hasn't gotten married! I don't know why. It hasn't been because of a lack of boyfriends, mind you," she said, holding up the finger of a wise woman. "I keep telling my daughters and grandchildren that there's no hurry to get married. The first priority should be to study, have a career, and get an income. Meanwhile, they shouldn't fall in love especially given how lost youth is nowadays. There are too many gold-diggers out there looking for child support," she said with pity, rubbing her fingers together as she mentioned money. "And don't get me started on boys. They get girls pregnant and disappear," she said, dismissing them with the palm of her hand, then poking Ciprián and raising her finger of wisdom again. "Before getting married, one must get to know well the other and be sure that it's the person one is willing to spend the rest of a lifetime with. My granddaughter made her career as an engineer like her mother. She was responsible by not getting pregnant in the meantime. Now she has to give me some great-grandsons!" she said, laughing out loud. "I'm ready to go to heaven but not before seeing my great-grandchildren. I can't leave!

While the old woman continued yapping, Ciprián, who naturally never took part in the conversation in the first place, stood up from his chair and walked away, continuing his wandering around the retirement home.

It must have been difficult for that poor girl to have her grandmother reminding her that she could only die after seeing her grandchildren. Maybe that's why she never visited. At that moment I asked myself: if for this woman seeing her great-grandchildren was her only reason to live, what kept the rest of those elderly people alive? What worse motivator than that of living in a retirement home, where everyone was fully conscious it would be the last place they would see before dying, where every other month one of them would disappear from the face of the earth?

Some of them were surely not enjoying at all the most miserable of joys that their hearts would let them feel. The well-dressed lady sang and danced happily among the other church ladies, but that was only that day. She would dress to impress daily, waiting for a relative to come, only to be disappointed. Perhaps the only thing she needed was a last visit from someone special, to be loved one last time before leaving. Close to her was also the bitter man on the wheelchair; he was making a dog's face, holding a paper with church songs on it as one of the church ladies took his hand and sang along with the rest of the happy elders. He also must have had something that was keeping him alive, even if that something was the fear of knowing where he would end up.

Ciprián made a stop in front of the balcony overlooking the mountains and got distracted by the landscape. Not far from where he was standing, there was a sofa in the corner where the couple with fifty-nine years of marriage sat. What kept them alive?

"Sweetheart, give me a minute. I have to go to the restroom," the old man said.

The man was surprised by a firm clutch by his wife, who looked at him out of the corner of her eye but was too weak to move. The man quickly kneeled in front of her and began kissing her, caressing her hands and hair. The whole of her emotions were almost completely restrained, present only through the faint tremble of her lips.

"Honey, I'm here. I'm not leaving you," the old man said with a smile on his face, convinced that he shouldn't expect a response from her but that she was still there listening. He talked to her not because of his own need to do it but because of her need to hear him.

"I love you..." his wife said, trying to catch her breath.

That couple passed away a few months after. The woman, although she suffered from the same condition as Ciprián, couldn't fight it anymore. Her body simply gave up. The man, as healthy as he seemed for his age, was also gone two or three days after his wife parted. It was said that death came to him because of his suffering. That couple was kept alive because of the love they felt for one another. They truly lived for one another.

I remember when Ciprián uttered those same three words to Margarita. I remember how her eyes got filled with joy and illusion upon hearing them. It must have been really difficult for her to lose Ciprián, to find that inside him was a man unknown to her, capable of harming her so much. Upon her disillusionment she must have given up. She must have lost her will to live.

There is absolutely nothing that can justify suicide. Her soul could have and should have done more for her. It had a whole life to help her face any hardship that steered her in the wrong path, to be strong and persist, to find happiness. It didn't do it. Her soul likewise gave up, but long before Margarita gave up on herself. It let her live a saint's life, protected by her home and family but without being exposed to the important things in life, those things from which one can learn, those things that could have enriched it.

Maybe Margarita had a young soul inside of her, a soul that knew little of how much power it had to influence, a soul that ignored what it was capable of doing with one life. Maybe it believed its job was to simply observe rather than grow. I don't blame it. I've been there myself. I had to learn the hard way.

"Ciprián! Again taking your clothes off in public? Who do you think you are? An exhibitionist?" a nurse shouted in front of the whole party of church volunteers as she rushed him to his room.

Because his clothes made his body itch, Ciprián developed the bad habit of taking them off and dispersing them piece by piece around the floor of the common area.

As the number of public display cases increased, it became routine for Quique to visit Ciprián at the retirement home and find him shirtless on the bed, on his knees, and with his diapers doing a pathetic job in covering his privates, jerking persistently the restraints that shackled him to the sides of his bed like an animal. He had always a cold stare, his face lacking any signs of the deep suffering and desperation he felt within, forced to keep silent as he kept being humiliated by his own body in rapid decadence.

Despite the horrid scene, Quique still had the courage to look at his father not with the pity and shame that he deserved, but with the admiration and respect a child always had for his father. Quique hadn't stopped believing Ciprián was still inside that body. Something kept making him come while the others had forgotten him; he hadn't given up.

To my surprise, one evening Quique sat in front of me, opened a red journal, and began to read.

"Weeks have passed and the dead man is still in my home..." Quique read on, losing himself within the pages of Margarita's diary.

Ciprián wouldn't stop fighting against his restraints; I wouldn't stop listening.

CHAPTER XVIII
Why?

My existence has now been reduced to witnessing, from a dark corner, how this body keeps accumulating so many hours of dead life. He's been lying down on this bed for years, struggling against his internal organs, which one after the other continue to cease operations. He has no more strength to move or to breathe. He's kept alive by lines that supply him with oxygen, food, and water, but that do no more than to prolong an empty existence; they keep me trapped here.

His mind and his sight have gotten lost in their own game of imposing memories into reality. The film, which years ago started by morphing whomever happened to be in front of him, now projects itself so quickly through his eyes that the only thing that remains is a pure white light, a mix of the colors that compose each fraction of his memories. As time has passed, the rest of his senses have gone adrift and disappeared. Being no longer able to feel the warm touch of a loved one, or perceive a sweet aroma, or hear the laugh of those dear to us, for what purpose does the body insist on sustaining life?

Despite all the years I've spent locked inside my own dark room, I can't stop thinking about the time when Quique read Margarita's diary to me. To this day, remembering the story of her life disturbs me not because of the life full of sorrows that she lived, but because of how much the soul inside of her must have suffered.

I arrived to the conclusion that her soul wasn't as young as I originally thought it to be. I had underestimated it. It was an old soul, much older than me. It must have been, because even with Margarita battling against it to stay within the boundaries of reality, it had managed to do things with her body that I never imagined possible. Discovering those powers made the demons from Ciprián's past invade my thoughts. How much suffering could I have prevented? Family? Friends? Acquaintances? Strangers? I've had to accept my guilt and make peace with all those demons. In that respect I have grown, being aware of how much more I will be capable of doing from the beginning of my next life.

However, something still makes me feel uneasy when I think about that old soul. What could have made it destroy Margarita's life? Why punish her with so much pain? Why force her to take her own life? I can find only one answer to these questions: desperation. It was an old soul but a lost soul, driven to desperation after accumulating under its belt hundreds of failed lives, hundreds of lives of supposed growth but that never resulted in transcendence. Facing perdition, it must have looked to innovate elsewhere, to experiment with the body, to accelerate life and death. It must have imagined that was the best way to cover more ground, reach the answers it desperately sought, and find the way out: the coveted white shoes.

Then I consider the world in which beings have to live. It is a vast world divided into societies that, since the origin of mankind, have defined what is good and what is evil according to the individual circumstances, precarious or abundant, in which they find themselves. Then comes the soul, citizen of the world, who upon encountering each new life is forced to leave behind antiquated goals and redefine them, convinced by the important changes that have taken place and by the special circumstances of each new reality, aided in its assimilation by others for the supposed common good.

Perhaps that is how Margarita's soul started its journey, learning new things life after life, re-learning things that were already known, and adapting to the supposed reality until it couldn't take it anymore. How many other souls must have consciously prevented its progress, likewise blinded by that vicious circle that controls their existences?

I may have been one of those wretched souls, in this life or in past ones. I've wanted to guide Ciprián through a path of success without defining success or the reason for wanting what that definition entails, through a path of happiness without defining happiness or the reason for wanting what that definition entails. I've let myself get carried away by the currents of life simply because it was easier that way, safer. I built my own world my way, but in the image of others, never forgetting to highlight my good deeds while doing my bad deeds in hiding. I annihilated dreams and desires of true importance because I never had them; I didn't dream them; I didn't desire them.

To this day, I hadn't realized that I had never questioned neither the motives for the path I have taken, nor the motives for the results I intended to have, nor how satisfied I was with myself as those two questions were answered. As must have been the case for Margarita's soul, I've gone from life to life believing that I've experienced both misery and glory, but measuring it all by the intensity and circumstances of the moment rather than by a motive. Without realizing this, wouldn't the logical conclusion be that after hundreds of failed lives, I too am destined to fall into the abyss of desperation? Could it be possible that a soul, a victim of the desperation caused by its circumstances, could go insane?

www.ingramcontent.com/pod-product-compliance
Lightning Source LLC
Chambersburg PA
CBHW022158260626
47155CB00019B/3086